The Girl from the Attic

The
Girl
from the
Attic

Marie Prins

COMMON DEER PRESS

Published by Common Deer Press Incorporated.

Copyright © 2020 Marie Prins

Published in 2020 by Common Deer Press
3203-1 Scott St.
Toronto, ON
M5E 1A1

Library of Congress Cataloging-in-Publication Data
Marie Prins—First edition.
The Girl from the Attic / Marie Prins
ISBN 978-1-988761-51-0 (print)
ISBN 978-1-988761-52-7 (e-book)

Cover Image and Interior Illustrations: Edward Hagedorn
Book Design: Siobhan Bothwell

First print July 2020, Second print October 2020
Printed in Canada

www.commondeerpress.com

To my mother, Alice Suzanne Wisse,
who taught me to read.

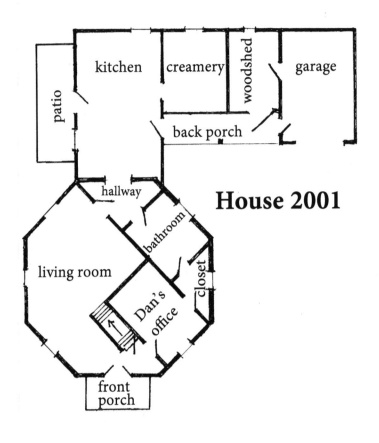

kitchen

creamery

woodshed

garage

patio

back porch

House 2001

hallway

living room

bathroom

closet

Dan's office

front porch

The Octagon House

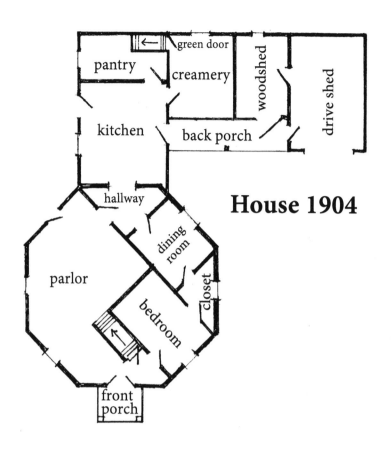

House 1904

- green door
- pantry
- creamery
- woodshed
- drive shed
- kitchen
- back porch
- hallway
- dining room
- parlor
- closet
- bedroom
- front porch

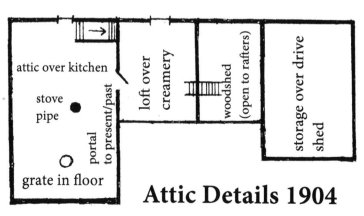

Attic Details 1904

- attic over kitchen
- loft over creamery
- woodshed (open to rafters)
- storage over drive shed
- stove pipe
- portal to present/past
- grate in floor

"Life can only be understood backwards; but it must be lived forwards." Søren Kierkegaard

Prologue
Spring 2001

The cat sat on the old windowsill, as she had off and on for a hundred years. Below, a green station wagon rumbled to a stop on the slushy road. A pale face peered out its rear window. The glass rolled down with fits and starts and a pair of green eyes squinted at the dilapidated house covered in dull red bricks, which were crumbling along its foundation. Instantly the cat crouched behind the curtain.

"You've got to be kidding!" a girl said, her voice sullen but penetrating. "We're going to live here? This place looks like a huge, moldy cupcake."

The man turned off the engine and unfolded his body from the car. With long strides, he stepped onto the uneven sidewalk towards the boxy front porch that sagged in one corner. Above, the cat slunk further into the shadows.

"It's an octagon, Maddy," the man said. He widened his

arms as if to embrace its eight sides. "Some guy built it a long time ago. In the 1800s. It was a wedding present for his wife."

"Too weird." *The girl slipped lower in her seat.*

The car's front window slid down. The cat watched a woman lift a camera to her eye and aim it at the house.

"It's an antique, hon," *the woman said as she snapped away.* "A very neglected one."

The man pulled on thick gloves. "It needs a lot of work. I'll start as soon as the sale closes and I get the keys."

The cat's eyes widened. She knew her long sleep was over. Just that morning, a cardinal wakened her with its song, and beneath the bird's feet, red buds on the maple branch swelled in the sunlight. Spring was arriving, and with it, this family. Now began the last undertaking before the cat could sleep forever.

From below, the man called over his shoulder. "C'mon, Maddy. Let's walk around the house." *He disappeared down the driveway.*

With her boot, the girl pushed open the car door and climbed out. A cold breeze blew a strand of red hair into her eyes. She coughed. The woman called after her.

"Maddy Rose, your scarf!"

The girl frowned and wound it around her neck. She followed the man to the side of the octagon. The cat jumped off the sill and sprinted to a window overlooking the driveway. It saw the woman adjust her camera lens and take more pictures before carefully stepping over ice patches on the concrete drive. The woman stopped and stared at the L-shaped, wooden building extending from the back of the octagon.

"What's that?" *she asked the man.*

"It's a kitchen with an enormous wood stove." *His voice*

was loud, exuberant. "You'll love it!" He waved his hand towards the shorter part of the L. "Next to it is a workroom! Your new studio! And here is the woodshed."

He swung open a crooked door. "It's full of junk now, but I'll stack it high with wood for the winter."

The cat smiled. Wood for the stove meant warmth for her old bones. Below, the woman, who'd left the car, leaned forward and glanced inside the woodshed. But the girl stood stock still, her arms pressed stiffly against her sides. The cat twitched its nose. Better pay attention, she thought. Woodsheds have lofts and lofts have secrets.

As the three people trekked around the back of the house, the cat dashed downstairs through the cold kitchen and into the workroom. She scratched open a small green door next to an old porcelain sink and bounded up narrow steps to a low-ceilinged room above the kitchen. From the sill of its only window, the cat surveyed the garden through its grimy glass. Below, the woman was talking excitedly to the man and taking pictures of withered cabbages that poked through thawing snow. The girl was kicking clumps of ice. She turned and trudged towards the maple trees on the south lawn. Halfway up the path, she wobbled on its slippery stones.

"Careful, Maddy!" the woman called out.

The girl turned and scowled. "You be careful too!" She pointed at the woman's swollen stomach.

Then she stamped her foot. "I can't believe we're moving to this creepy place in the middle of nowhere!" Without waiting for a reply, she stamped around the corner and out of sight.

With a rare burst of energy, the cat streaked back to the front upstairs window and pressed herself against the glass. She watched the girl climb into the back seat of the car and *slam the door. The cat's eyes narrowed.* She needs to know this house's stories, *she growled in a purring sort of way. The old stories. The hard ones too.*

Below, the girl shifted in her seat and stared at the upstairs window. The cat stared back. As the girl's eyes widened, she flicked the white tip of her tail like the flame of an old, tapered candle pulling the girl towards its light.

Chapter 1
Early Summer 2001

Crack! An egg slid out of its shell and disappeared into the bowl. *Crack!* The dry pancake flour swallowed another. Sitting with folded arms at the kitchen table, Maddy watched her mother beat the mixture and pour its lumpy batter onto a sizzling grill.

Amy was right. Eggs and promises were meant to be broken. The last time Maddy's mother, Carla, had whipped up a pancake breakfast, they had lived in a bungalow in Scarborough. Then she married Dan. Despite their promise to stay in the city until Maddy's twelfth birthday, here she was, hunched over an empty plate under the peak of a high wooden ceiling in a huge kitchen over a hundred kilometers away. It felt like the other side of the world.

"With the baby coming, we need a bigger house," her mother had explained. "Don't worry, you'll like living in the country. All that fresh air. It'll get rid of the cough that's plagued you all winter. Maybe help clear up your asthma too. And soon you'll have a new sister. How wonderful is that?"

Maddy didn't really think it was wonderful at all. She didn't like babies, with their wobbly necks and all their fussing. She'd probably end up babysitting all the time. At least, that's what her best friend Amy had predicted—*You'll see. They'll break their promises. Before you know it, you'll be changing dirty diapers!*

Carla flipped a pancake in the cast-iron frying pan and tapped it down with the spatula. Its buttery smell filled the air. Maddy's misery melted as she stared out the picture window by the table.

A beam of summer sun filled the syrup jar with an amber light. Maddy poured a puddle of its golden sweetness onto her plate. As she traced circles in the syrup, she squinted into the bright sunshine outdoors. Beyond the patio, shadows danced under the maple tree. A chipmunk ran up the trunk. In a wink, a long black tail with a white tip vanished into the bushes.

"Hey Mom! Did Dan find any cats when he was fixing up this place?"

"Not that he mentioned." Carla slipped the hot pancakes onto Maddy's plate.

Maddy frowned. Dan wouldn't mention finding a cat. He didn't like them. Said they would make her asthma worse. Her mother thought she could get a cat from the Humane Society as soon as they moved, but that was another promise bound to be broken. Dan would convince her that he was right.

The back door banged open and Dan stomped into the large kitchen.

"Boots off!" commanded Carla.

"No worries, I'm leaving right away! Gotta get to the dump with the junk from the woodshed."

Maddy cut a pancake into quarters and folded one into her mouth.

"After the dump, it's the woodlot for firewood. Want to come, Maddy?"

Maddy swallowed. Really? Go to the dump and then tramp through the woods all day? She'd rather be on MSN with Amy planning her escape from this weird place. Covering her mouth, she pretended to cough.

Dan reached for his coffee mug and leather gloves. "Ahh, your cough! Well, maybe next time." He nudged open the door with his boot. "Maddy, with the baby coming, your mother could use your help around here." Eyebrows raised, he sent her a knowing look before the door snapped shut behind him.

Maddy glanced at her mother who was patting her stomach as she gazed out the window by the sink. Maddy knew she wouldn't be able to fool her. With a sigh, she poked at the last pancake. It was round like her mother's belly. Feeling suddenly full, she pushed the plate away.

"Dan's right, Maddy Rose!" Carla turned around. "I need help in the garden. Time to get dressed."

Maddy groaned. She hated pulling weeds. How was she going to escape this one? With a scowl, she dragged her feet through the living room and past the den. Inside, Dan's new blue iMac sparkled on his desk. Maddy eyed it. She wondered if Amy was online and whether or not Dan had changed the password again. Perhaps if she disappeared for a while, her mother would forget about her and she'd have time to go online. Upstairs in her room, Maddy stripped off her pajamas and tugged on a T-shirt and jeans. Back at the bottom of the stairs, she edged open the front door, careful not to rattle its loose, antique knob.

Moments later, she heard the kitchen screen door bang shut. Maddy waited a minute for Carla to make her way into the backyard and then snuck around the octagon to the woodshed. She silently swung open its heavy, wooden door.

A dull shaft of daylight seeped through a small window cut high in the back wall. It revealed a loft stretching above her head into the shadows. The perfect hiding place! Bracing a ladder against the wall, Maddy climbed over its top rung and scrambled onto a dusty floor. Under the window sat a worn captain's chair. Maddy sank into its seat and, bracing an elbow on its arm, propped her chin in her hand.

Living in the country was soooo boring. The TV had only three channels. The VCR was broken and Dan refused to upgrade to a DVD player. And, worst of all, she could only use Dan's computer when he gave her permission, which was once in a blue moon. Totally unfair.

Even then, chatting with Amy on MSN messenger was nearly impossible. It took forever to download anything with the abysmal, dial-up internet. Basically, she was stranded on a desert island. Except there was no sand, no beach. Just a round house and two dumb acres in the land of nowhere.

The whole situation, she concluded, was Dan's fault. Dan the Man. That's what Amy called him. Carla had said things wouldn't change after he moved into their house in the city. But they sure had. Like, right away. First he took up way too much space because he was such a big guy—like, he wore size thirteen boots! Then he piled his stuff everywhere. Even stored his tools in her mother's studio. Then he married her. And then she got pregnant. Or maybe it was the other way around. She certainly didn't want to think about that. But no matter, because right away Dan convinced her mom to buy this house on the edge of Colebrook, far from its downtown block of stores. Which was as weird as building an octagon for a wedding present, like that guy did for his wife over a hundred years ago. And now all Dan the Man did was eat! Like a huge carpenter ant. "We'll plant a big vegetable garden in back," her mother had gushed when the house sale closed. "Carrots, potatoes, zucchini. You name it!" Now she was always tired, and she needed Maddy's help . . . like, all the time.

As Maddy's eyes adjusted to the darkness of the loft, she spotted a brown trunk in the back corner. She crept towards it and pushed on its rounded lid. It didn't budge. She banged its rusty latch. Dust spiraled into the air. She sneezed and banged again. The lid slipped sideways a sliver. With a heave, she lifted it and peered inside.

In the faint light, Maddy recognized the hunched shape of a black cat stitched onto a quilt. Faded yellow eyes peered back at her. Cautiously, she touched the cloth. The white tip of its tail twitched. She yelped and fell backward with a hard thump.

Chapter 2

The cat in the bushes!

Maddy scrambled to her feet. She bent over the trunk. Nothing moved. She stared at the cat for a long moment, then took a deep breath and tugged the quilt all the way out. More dust and a faint musty smell rose out of its folds. Maddy sneezed. Nose twitching, she bunched the quilt in her arms and draped it over the back of the captain's chair. She could see that its edges were frayed and a mouse had chewed a hole in one corner. A ray of light from the window spot lit a large red barn stitched in the middle. Farm animals circled around it—a rooster, three hens, two cows, a black horse, and a black cat with a white tip on its tail.

Maddy brushed her finger over the cat. Again, its tail twitched. She jerked back as if it had bitten her. But then she noticed a worn, loose thread. She smiled. The cat did not. It sat still, its yellow eyes unblinking.

A shiver of excitement ran up Maddy's spine. Someone

who'd lived in this house had probably sewn this quilt a long time ago. Did her mother know about it? Apparently not. She was a photographer. If she'd known, she'd already have hung it up somewhere and taken a dozen pictures of it for a country craft magazine.

"Maddy Rose, where are you?" Her mother's voice floated up through the floor of the loft. It sounded like she was standing right below her. Maddy quickly folded the quilt, making sure the cat lay on top, and shoved it in the trunk. With a determined heave, she pushed the trunk further into the corner. Then she climbed down the ladder, left the woodshed, and slipped back into the kitchen.

Her mother stood at the sink rinsing lettuce and spinach leaves.

"What's up?" Maddy asked nonchalantly.

Carla raised an eyebrow. "Where have you been? You didn't show up in the garden."

Maddy shrugged. "Getting dressed."

"C'mon, Maddy. I really do need your help. There's stew to be made for supper. But first," she tilted her head and waved a hand in the air. "I want to tackle this ceiling. Look at those cobwebs!"

Maddy crossed her arms and shifted her weight to one leg. She eyed the wide pine boards high above her head. For the first time, she noticed a fringe of grimy dust covering the blades of a ceiling fan.

Her mother shook her head. "What possessed Leo to put a cathedral ceiling in this kitchen? It's impossible to dust without ladders and a long extension on the vacuum cleaner."

"Who's Leo?" Maddy asked in her best flat voice.

"The guy who owned this house before us. I wish he hadn't . . ." her mother's words trailed away as her hands circled her stomach.

"I'm tired," Maddy grumbled.

Carla raised both eyebrows. Maddy sighed and trudged into the workroom next to the kitchen. It was an odd room, with rough, planked walls painted a dull red. Dan called it a creamery. He claimed that ages ago the farmer had separated cream from milk in this workroom before storing it in large metal cans. That now made sense to Maddy. The quilt in the trunk had a big barn and two cows stitched on it. She glanced at the narrow white boards on the ceiling. The loft and the trunk must be right above her head. No wonder she heard her mother's voice so clearly moments ago.

Maddy circled past one of Dan's toolboxes and pulled open the door to the storage closet next to the washing machine. When she reached for the vacuum cleaner, she noticed the back wall of the closet was made from a green wooden panel. Even though there was no knob, Maddy thought it looked like a door. But leading to where? Not another room, for her mother stood in the kitchen on the other side of that wall and its green panel.

While Carla positioned a ladder and climbed its steps, Maddy lifted the vacuum cleaner off the floor. With one awkward swipe after another, her mother sucked dust off the fan's blades and spider webs from the pine boards above their heads. Maddy's arms ached. A sticky gob of dust fell onto her cheek. She hunched her shoulders and tried to wipe it off. A tickle rose in her throat. She began to cough. Was her asthma going to kick in? Maddy coughed again. If she pretended to wheeze, maybe her mother would take pity on her and stop vacuuming. But her mother ignored Maddy's coughs and kept working. At last, she stepped off the ladder and sank into a chair.

"Thank goodness that's done! I'm exhausted!" She wiped sweat from her forehead. "Maddy, hon, check the mailbox. I'm waiting for my last contract before the baby arrives."

For the first time, Maddy noticed the dark circles under her mother's eyes. She really did look exhausted. A lot more than Maddy's pretend tiredness.

"Okay, no prob," Maddy said, surprised at her sudden willingness to help but a little worried by the way her mother had slumped into her chair.

As she walked towards the mailbox, a car backed out of the neighbor's driveway across the road. It rolled slowly past the octagon before driving off. Behind the steering wheel, a small woman with white hair and dark eyes peered at Maddy through gold-rimmed glasses. She looked as ancient as their house.

In the mailbox, instead of a letter for her mother, there was a large envelope addressed to Madison Rose Stevens. It had Poppa George's return address, her old house in Scarborough. The house her grandfather had moved into after they left. The one Maddy had begged to live in with him when her mother and Dan announced their plans to move to the country.

Maddy sat down on the front porch steps, opened the envelope, and pulled out a copy of *Country Farms* magazine from 1985. On its cover was a yellow sticky note that read, *Found this in The Antique Shoppe. Check out pp. 10 & 12.*

Maddy grinned. Poppa George enjoyed rummaging through junk shops and sharing his finds with her. He was a retired high school teacher who loved to tell stories about local history. When she lived in her old house, close to downtown Toronto, he had told her about the secret passages in Casa Loma and the ghosts in the government buildings at Queen's Park, often adding spooky noises to scare her.

Curious about his latest discovery, Maddy thumbed to page ten in the magazine. On it was a colored photograph of a bright, red brick octagon with a small, tidy front porch. Underneath it, she read the yellow-highlighted words, *Built in the 1850's, this unusually shaped house still stands on the eastern edge of Colebrook, close to the shores of Lake Ontario.*

"Wow!" Maddy exclaimed. "That's our house!" She frowned. It looked so different with white trim and rose-colored glass brightening the front door. Leaning against the porch pillar, she began to read the article. Suddenly, a black cat circled past her and down the driveway. Maddy blinked. Then she shoved the magazine under the doormat and sprinted around the house in time to see a black tail with a white tip disappear into the woodshed. When she yanked open the door, the cat scooted up the ladder into the loft.

Without flicking on the light switch, Maddy followed it into the darkness. In the dim light from the window, she recognized the shape of the trunk. But now, in the low back wall, a faint glow shone around the sides of a small, rectangular door.

Maddy crept towards its outline. She bent down for a better look. An old-fashioned iron latch beckoned her to lift it and tug on the handle below. Without a sound, the door swung open.

Chapter 3

Maddy stooped through the small door into a long room with low walls and a sloping ceiling. It looked like one of the junk shops Poppa George explored with her. There was a jumble of old furniture—a mattress on an iron bed frame, a washstand with a cracked, oval mirror, a long, rolled up rug. She hadn't seen this room when she first explored the octagon after their move. Was it part of the woodshed? If so, why hadn't Dan hauled all this junk to the dump?

Something landed with a thud in the shadows. The cat! Where was she? Maddy stepped forward to look under the bed and stumbled. When she regained her balance, she realized that she'd almost fallen down a flight of stairs. Heart thumping, she peered down steep steps that led to a narrow, green door and two yellow eyes that blinked and vanished.

Maddy shrank away from the stairs. Was the cat down there? Or something else? Shivers, like mice feet, ran up her spine. Then she felt her back grow warm. Heat radiated from a fat, black pipe rising through the floor in the middle of the room to the ceiling. A few feet away, a faint pattern of light shimmered out of an iron grate in the floor.

Through it came a low murmur of voices that grew louder and more distinct, as if an invisible hand had adjusted a radio to its right spot.

"The bread's out of the oven. I'll butter the carrots now."

"That pot is heavy. Let me drain and mash the potatoes."

"Are the sausages done yet?"

In a room below, muffled footsteps crossed the floor. A lid clanked on a pot. The steely rasp of a knife being sharpened rose through the grate. More footsteps. A moment later, Maddy heard a blade scratching a wooden surface with repetitive strokes.

She crept to the grate and knelt over it. At first, through its geometric pattern, she saw only a long table covered in a white cloth. On top sat five plates and cups. In the middle, slices of bread cooled on a cutting board. A yeasty aroma drifted up to Maddy's nose. Then a small, hunched woman, dressed in black from head to toe shuffled to the table and placed a bowl of steaming carrots in its middle.

Maddy twisted her head and leaned closer to the grate. A large black cookstove came into view. Sausages and onions sizzled in a frying pan at its back. Next to it, steam rose lazily out of an iron kettle. In front of the stove, stood a tall, young woman with her hair pinned on top of her head. She grasped the handle of a large pot and vigorously mashed the potatoes in it.

Maddy inched her knees sideways and peered into the corner of the old kitchen. There sat a black rocking chair with bright purple and white asters painted on its back. Behind it stretched a red brick wall. Maddy sucked in her breath in astonishment.

"That's the wall in my kitchen!"

She clapped her hand over her mouth. The bent woman tilted her head sideways and glanced at the ceiling.

Maddy leaned away from the grate, afraid she had been seen by the strangers below her. What were they doing in her kitchen? And why did it look so different? When she peered again through the opening, she saw the old woman wave her hand towards the back door where a rusty squeaking of metal against metal could be heard outside.

"I hear them washing up at the pump, Helen."

"Then sit yourself down, Aunt Ella, and I'll finish the serving." The young woman adjusted a white apron over her long gray and white striped skirt. Why were they wearing those clothes in the summer? They looked awfully hot.

As Aunt Ella plumped a pillow in a chair by the table, boots stomped across the wooden floor. Maddy's nose touched the grate as she bent closer to see the new arrivals. A long-legged boy and a heavy-set man with dark cropped hair entered the kitchen, scraped their chairs over the wooden floor, and settled down at the table below her.

"Where's Eva?" asked Aunt Ella, a note of concern in her voice.

"In the hen house," the boy said. "One of the new chicks is looking sickly. She's fixing a box for it."

"Oh, Clare, shouldn't you be giving her a hand?"

Clare rose in his chair, but before he could stand, a tall, thin girl with brown curls framing a flushed face burst through the door. She held a wooden box. Straw poked over its edges. From inside came a weak *peep-peep*.

"This chick needs a warm place!" Eva pushed the box next to the cookstove's metal legs. She straightened and wiped her hands on her skirt.

A dark shape slunk from under the table and disappeared behind the stove.

"The cat'll get it!" said Aunt Ella.

With a serene smile, Eva shook her head and sat down next to Clare.

"Shadow's just curious." On cue, the black cat with the white tip on its tail sniffed the box and retreated back under Aunt Ella's chair. Eva laughed and picked up her fork.

"To be safe, Clare says he'll put a lid on the box. And he'll feed the chick for me and change its water after I leave. I named it Speckles. After the marks on its feathers."

"Best not get a liking for it," said the older man. "You won't be wanting to eat a chicken that you've named."

"Oh, Uncle Ray, we're not going to eat it! It's a laying hen."

Clare shifted in his chair. "That little peeper may be a rooster, Eva."

Eva took a bite of carrot and chewed it slowly.

"Perhaps," she said softly. "But still, it deserves to live."

Aunt Ella regarded Eva with sad eyes but said nothing. Clare stared at his plate. For a few minutes no one spoke. Then Eva covered her mouth and coughed into her hand, a short, tight cough. She put down her fork.

"I'm not hungry," she said. "I think I'll rest till it's time for the train."

Clare jumped up and pulled the rocking chair away from the wall. When Eva sat down, she began to cough again. Reaching into her skirt pocket, she pulled out a large handkerchief and buried her face in it. A long spasm racked her body. When it stopped, a large red stain spread across the white cloth she held in her hands.

Chapter 4

Maddy edged away from the grate. She felt light-headed from bending over for so long. Below, voices filled with alarm gave directions to fetch another handkerchief, a blanket, a cup of tea. Footsteps rushed back and forth.

As she listened to the commotion downstairs, flashbacks of her own coughing fits flared up in her head. They had often left her breathless. Once a small spot of blood had tinged her own tissue pink. But never bright red.

A dry tickle began to grow and burn in Maddy's throat. Desperate for water, she stumbled through the small door into the woodshed loft, slid down its ladder, and raced to the sink in the kitchen of her own time which now seemed strangely quiet. There was no sign of the family who had been sharing a meal there only moments ago. As she gulped mouthfuls of water, her throat relaxed. She exhaled a shaky breath and looked up at the cathedral ceiling. Her thoughts whirled round and round like the fan blades suspended high above her head. Was the room she fled really up there? But how? Dan had said just the other day that he hoped there was enough insulation above the pine boards to fill the space right to the roof and keep them warm in the winter.

Maddy glanced at the brick wall across the room. A shadow wavered like the sway of a rocking chair. Prickles ran up her arms. A figure in a long robe stepped into the small, dark hallway between the kitchen and the octagon's living room. Maddy gasped.

"What's wrong?" Her mother stopped abruptly in the doorway.

Maddy blinked. "N-n-nothing," she said. "You . . . you scared me."

Carla pulled her bathrobe around her protruding stomach. "I just took a shower, hon. Haven't dried my hair yet. Any letters in the mailbox?"

The mailbox? Maddy had completely forgotten about it. She shook her head.

"Too bad." Her mother's shoulders sagged as she pushed the damp hair off her forehead. "Cleaning that ceiling tuckered me out, Maddy. I think I need a nap." She turned and padded slowly across the living room floor.

Maddy listened to her mother's tired footsteps mount the stairs and shuffle over the bedroom carpet. Seconds later, she heard the squeak of bed springs, followed by the soft thud of slippers hitting the floor.

She wanted to shout that something weird was going on in their house. But she didn't call out. Her mother looked exhausted. And there was no way she would believe

Maddy's story. No one would. Probably not even Amy. She'd say the octagon was making her crazy.

Was it? Or was she hallucinating again, like when she was delirious with a high fever last winter? Maddy felt her forehead. It was warm. So were her cheeks. Maybe . . . but no, she felt fine, just very confused. She stared at the ceiling. Was she living in a house like those places Poppa George had told her about, the ones with secret passages and ghosts? She shivered. Was that why he had sent her the magazine? To let her in on a secret about the octagon?

Maddy hesitantly tiptoed through the living room to the front door. She pulled out the magazine from under the doormat and, feeling her knees wobble, sat down slowly to read the article.

In 1853, Robert Sanders built the octagon as a wedding gift for his wife Martha. It wasn't a fancy house like the ones in town. Its rooms, while odd shapes, were plain. There were no carved moldings around the doors or leaded glass in its windows. After all, the Sanders were farmers. They had no money for extras. Later, a two-story addition was added to the back of the octagon. It housed a kitchen and pantry. Upstairs was an attic where the hired hands slept in the warmer months.

"That's where I was!" Maddy exclaimed. "In the attic! But it's not there anymore!" There was barely room above the kitchen ceiling for squirrels or mice.

Maddy read on. The next paragraph in the article explained that the current owner was modernizing the octagon. He had dug a basement beneath it and had torn out the attic room above the kitchen and installed a cathedral ceiling using old pine boards rescued from the railroad station torn down in Colebrook. "Oh," Maddy whispered. "That explains how a whole floor disappeared, but not how I found myself inside it a half hour ago."

She dropped her head into her hands and rubbed her forehead trying to make sense of it all. Her stomach felt like it had just jumped over a speed bump while racing her bike down the road. She remembered reading books about time travel to faraway planets and even one into the past through an old root cellar dug behind an ancient house like hers. Had she somehow stumbled through a portal into an old attic that no longer existed? Into an older time in her own house? But those books were only stories. People really didn't travel through time. Such a thing was incredulous, even scary. But Maddy sensed it could also be super exciting.

Maddy quickly turned the page of the magazine and discovered another mystery: a photograph of a red barn that sat high on a stone foundation. Underneath it she read, *Across from the octagon stands a large barn with stalls for horses and cows.* A few short sentences described the crops the Sanders grew and how they raised chickens and sold eggs. The article concluded that, unfortunately, just before the magazine went to press, the barn had burned down.

Maddy rubbed at the chill on her arms. She clearly remembered seeing a barn on the old quilt in the trunk. And a horse, and a cow, and chickens.

She guessed that her house must have been a farmhouse once upon a time. And that the people eating dinner in the old kitchen were probably the Sanders. The man dressed in overalls sure looked like a farmer. The boy too, although Maddy hadn't seen him clearly through the grate. And the girl called Eva had had a little chicken in a box. . . .

Maddy suspected that, somehow, she really had traveled back in time. Though she had no clue how that had happened, she felt calmer. At least she knew the attic room had once existed. That she hadn't made it up. In fact, there was a small door in the woodshed that led to it. Next to that door was a trunk, and in that trunk was a quilt with that farm scene stitched on it. Maddy took a shaky breath and stood up. She needed to lift the lid on the trunk and touch the quilt just to make sure that she wasn't crazy or hallucinating. Then maybe she could gather her courage and open the door to the attic again.

Maddy tucked the magazine back under the doormat and walked resolutely to the woodshed. From the top rung of the ladder, she saw the captain's chair and spotted the trunk in the corner, but one glance around the loft told her the small door at its back had vanished.

Maddy hesitated and then crept past the trunk to the wall. She felt along it for the iron latch. Nothing. She pressed the boards with her open palms. They didn't budge. Bewildered, she sank onto the trunk. With a click, its lock popped up and poked her leg. She stood and lifted the lid. The cloth cat on the quilt stared at her, its yellow eyes unblinking, its tail perfectly still.

For a moment, Maddy stared back. Was this the cat she saw in the old kitchen? The one they called Shadow? She gently touched its head before cautiously pushing the quilt aside. Underneath, her fingers brushed against a small rag doll wedged into the corner of the trunk. It was slightly bigger than her hand. Two braids of brown yarn framed a painted oval face with blue eyes, a small curve of a nose, and a tiny, red mouth. Its soft body wore a simple, yellow dress and a white apron. Maddy had little interest in dolls, but this one had a sweet look on its face that tugged at her heart. She straightened its braids, fluffed up its wrinkled clothes, and placed it on top of the quilt next to the cat. Then she shut the lid of the trunk and slumped against it. With her shoe, she dejectedly scuffed at the dusty floor. She glanced at the back wall. Things weren't making sense. That small door to the attic had been there less than an hour ago. Why had it vanished? Had she been hallucinating? Or was she just plain crazy?

Maddy closed her eyes and listened to the flies buzzing in the window. In the hot air of the loft, she felt drowsy, her arms and legs heavy, almost too tired to move. She bunched up her knees and rested her head against them. The hum of flies grew louder and then faded away as she fell asleep.

Moments later, or maybe longer, fur brushed lightly against her legs. She jerked awake.

Chapter 5

The black cat padded away from her and towards the small door at the back of the loft. Maddy scrambled after it. Her hand shook as she lifted the iron latch and pushed it open. There was the attic room again! Looking carefully to both sides, she stepped inside. Directly in front of her, the cat crouched at the foot of the bed, kneading a folded, wool blanket with her front paws.

"Pssst, Shadow, we're back in the attic!" Maddy cocked her head and listened for noises. All was quiet. She stepped forward to scratch the cat's head, but it sprang off the bed and slunk across the room.

Maddy turned and gazed around her. This time she noticed a dress with long sleeves and a straw hat that hung on a hook by the small door. Further along the wall, she saw an old pair of metal skates dangling from a nail. In a far corner, a rocking horse nodded at her. In another stood a small wicker doll carriage with a missing wheel. The cat was crouching underneath it. In a flash, she darted past Maddy and leapt down the attic's narrow flight of stairs.

Maddy tiptoed to their edge. A sliver of light from below illuminated the steep steps and the green door at the bottom. Should she? Well, why not? Heart racing, she slowly climbed down. Her foot bumped the door. It swung open without a sound.

The downstairs room looked familiar and foreign at the same time. The walls had the identical dull, red paint as the room next to her own kitchen, the one Dan called the creamery. Its ceiling had the same narrow boards. But in place of Carla's washing machine and dryer, a shiny white, porcelain sink half full of water stretched along the wall. In it sat three metal pails full of milk with a layer of white stuff floating on top. Maddy poked her finger at one. Cream? She licked it. Yes!

Something moved by her feet. She sprang back, then relaxed when she saw two eyes blinking under the sink.

"Want a taste?" She dipped her finger in the pail and held out her hand. Ignoring the offer, Shadow marched to the door on the other side of the sink and meowed. When Maddy cracked it open, the cat scooted through. Maddy pushed the door open a bit further and peered into the room.

There was the large black cookstove. On top, steam rose lazily from an iron kettle. Late afternoon sun flickered through the window above a long table on which a white china teapot sat, its round sides painted with delicate pink apple blossoms. Next to its matching cups was a plate of sliced bread and a pot of jam. Maddy's stomach rumbled. It seemed like ages since she had eaten anything.

Without a sound, she stepped into the kitchen towards the table. Straightaway, she spotted an old woman dozing in the rocking chair by the red brick wall. Maddy froze. At the same time, the cat streaked across the floor and jumped into the woman's lap. A ball of blue wool rolled onto the floor.

"Shadow!" the woman exclaimed. Then she saw Maddy and her piercing eyes widened in recognition.

"You've come!"

Goose-bumps ran up Maddy's arms. She shrank back towards the creamery.

"Don't leave," the woman implored. "I've been awaiting you." Nudging the cat from her lap, she struggled from the rocking chair and rubbed her back. "I get stiff sitting so long."

She slowly picked up the ball of wool and tucked it in her apron pocket. Without fully straightening, she shuffled towards the cookstove, closer and closer to Maddy, who remained rooted to the floor as if hypnotized by the woman's bright eyes and hunched back. Knowing it was impolite to stare, Maddy quickly dropped her gaze.

The woman waved her hand in the air as if to shoo away a fly. "No need to be afraid!"

She plucked a thick potholder from the side of the stove and held it out to Maddy. "I need your help. They'll be wanting their tea."

She carefully set the china teapot on the edge of the stove. With a thin finger, she gestured for Maddy to pour the steaming water. Speechless, Maddy stared at the woman. Why in the world would she be waiting for her to pour a kettle of hot water? The woman returned her gaze with a brisk nod. Maddy shifted her weight from one foot to another, undecided about what to do. Then she took three steps to the stove. She lifted the heavy kettle and poured until the teapot overflowed. Drops of water danced and hissed on the hot metal. With a clunk, she dropped the kettle back onto the stovetop.

The woman smiled. "'Tis very full, but no matter." She spread butter and jam on two slices of bread and placed them next to teacups on saucers. With unsteady hands, she poured the tea and offered a cup to Maddy. "Sit a spell, girl, so's you can drink your tea."

Maddy didn't like tea, but she took the china cup anyway. In the corner, the bent woman lowered herself into the rocking chair. Maddy glanced at her. She seemed friendly enough, not as frightening as Maddy first thought. Maybe she just needed a little help with the kettle. No big deal. Besides, the smell of raspberry jam made Maddy's mouth water. With her foot, she nudged a chair from the table and perched on its edge. For a moment all was quiet in the room. Maddy stared into the teacup and then traced the apple blossom on its side. At her feet, the cat rubbed against her legs. Maddy set the teacup on the table and stroked the cat's thick fur.

"I heard you creaking in the attic, child. What's your name?"

The old woman's voice startled Maddy. She felt her cheeks grow warm. "Uh, Maddy," she stammered. "Madison Rose. But everyone calls me Maddy."

"Ah," the woman's eyes twinkled. "Your name is Rose. Like mine, Rosellen. But my family calls me Ella. Aunt Ella." She sipped the tea from her cup and set it on her stool.

"Sometimes I see you in my dreams, girl, drifting in and out of these rooms. It's the second sight I have . . . seeing things no one else sees. My Gran said it was done in the old country. But nowadays most folks won't hear of it."

Maddy shifted uneasily on her chair. She wasn't surprised that Aunt Ella could see into the future. In a movie she had watched recently, an old woman had peered into fire that revealed visions. But Maddy didn't know how to feel about someone seeing her in dreams.

Maddy swallowed a bite of the bread and jam but said nothing.

"'Tis strange . . . seeing folks come and go. Hard sometimes to know if they's real. At first, I thought you to be Eva, come back for a visit."

Maddy stopped chewing. "Come back? I just saw her this morning. She had a baby chick in a box." Maddy peered under the stove, but the box was gone.

For a moment Aunt Ella looked puzzled. Then she nodded, "Time speeds up, my child . . . and oft slows down." She picked up her knitting needles from the basket beside the rocking chair, unrolled a length of blue wool, and began to knit with a soft, steady rhythm.

"Eva lives with her mother, my niece Martha, in Belleville. When the weather warms, she comes for a visit. But last week, she went home early . . . on account of her illness."

The bright red stain on the handkerchief flashed through Maddy's mind.

"'Tis a hard thing to beat, consumption. I had it when I was a wee child. Twisted my spine, it did. But most folks have the coughing kind . . . like Eva. Always coughing and

31

coughing."

Maddy stiffened. Wait a minute! All winter she too had coughed a lot. From her asthma and bouts of bronchitis. At least that's what the doctor told her.

Aunt Ella turned the needles in her hands and shook her head. "'Tis always the same thing with consumption. They have a fever that comes and goes."

Maddy's fever had come and gone too. She touched her forehead to see if it was hot.

The needles started to click again.

"And with the coughing, they spit up blood."

Outside a dark cloud covered the sun and sent shadows into the room. A nibble of bread lumped in Maddy's throat. Twice, after lots of coughing, there had been blood in her tissue. With exaggerated effort, she swallowed her last bite of bread.

"Some get better." Click, click went the needles. "But some don't."

Maddy's head began to buzz, like flies trapped in a bottle. What was this old woman telling her? That she might have con . . . con . . . something? That coughing disease? A horrible thought skittered through her head. Was Aunt Ella, with her second sight, hinting that she could die too?

All of a sudden, Maddy felt her chest tighten. She tried to inhale, but now her breath stuck in her throat. She couldn't breathe. She sprang up and bolted into the creamery, up the steep steps, and into the attic. She went through the small door into the woodshed, back, safely she hoped, into her own time.

Chapter 6

Moments later, Maddy sank into a chair in the shade of the maple tree by the patio. She inhaled mouthfuls of cool air until her heart stopped racing and the tightness in her throat eased. She rubbed her arms to chase away the chill. Nothing made sense to her. Not the cat nor the quilt. Not the small attic door that she hoped didn't exist. Certainly not that hunch-backed woman telling her about a coughing disease that came with fevers and left and came back again. And maybe even led to . . . Maddy shuddered, afraid to follow her last thought further.

A telephone's shrill ring pierced the silence. Maddy waited for her mother to answer it. But after five rings, she pushed open the screen door and grabbed the receiver.

"Maddy!" boomed Poppa George.

Maddy cupped her hand over the mouthpiece. "Poppa, this house is too weird! You've got to come get me!"

"Speak up Maddy! I can't hear you. Did you get the magazine I sent?"

"Yes, Poppa." Was he wearing his hearing aids?

"Good, good." Her grandfather barreled on. "Did you know that the octagon was an unusual building even in its own time?"

No kidding. Maddy grimaced. So were the people who lived here. She flicked the long telephone cord up and down. Should she tell him about the old woman? If he knew there were ghosts living here, he'd let her move back to her old house with him.

"In the 1800s," Poppa George continued, "people believed that round houses were the perfect shape for promoting good health."

Really? With a despairing sigh, Maddy flopped onto the small sofa by the brick wall and wrapped the phone cord around her knees. Poppa was on another history roll. She had no choice but to hear him out.

"Folks believed that bad air and evil gathered in the corners of square rooms. In a round house, they would pass right through. Then people wouldn't get sick and die. It must have worked, because all eight of the Sanders children grew up to adulthood."

In her mind, Maddy saw Eva bent over in the rocking chair, coughing and coughing into a big white handkerchief. "This whole house isn't round, Poppa. This kitchen is a big rectangle. I bet bad air gets stuck here all the time. Like those cobwebs on the ceiling."

"That cathedral ceiling didn't exist a hundred years ago, Maddy. That article I sent you said the kitchen had an attic above it."

"Well, it did, Poppa! And if you climb up into the wood-shed loft—"

Maddy felt a jerk on the taut telephone cord. Behind her Carla raised it over her head and stepped through the doorway. Maddy jumped up.

"Gotta go, Poppa. Bye." She thrust the receiver at her mother and bent down, pretending to tie her shoelaces while she listened to Carla's weary voice ask about her grandfather's health.

"Come for a visit, Dad. Before I'm too tired to cook you a meal."

When her mother hung up, she said, "Maddy, I need beef boullion cubes for the stew. Think you could go to town and buy a package?"

"Like how?"

"Your bike. Dan put it in the garage."

"That old thing? I haven't ridden it since last summer!" Maddy frowned. She was tired too. But one glance at her mother's pale face changed her mind. "Got any money?"

Carla scooped change off the kitchen table and held out her hand. Maddy shoved the coins into her pocket. Then she tucked her puffer in on top. In the garage, she flicked on the light. Its dull beam reflected off the metal bumper of her bike, which was propped against the wall. She wheeled it into the driveway, dusted its seat, and rapidly turned its pedals a few times.

Then she squeezed its brakes. They seemed stiff, but they appeared to work. With an uncertain hop onto its seat, she wobbled down the driveway into the road and past a row of brick bungalows.

By the time she reached the corner, Maddy felt sure of

her balance and turned onto the county road towards the village of Colebrook. As she pedled in the shade of willow trees, the click of the bicycle's chain sounded like Aunt Ella's knitting needles. All of a sudden, exhaustion swooped down and tightened around her chest. Maybe she really did have that coughing disease. It was getting harder to breathe as she biked. She stopped pedling and coasted past a church and a dozen white clapboard houses until she reached the place where stores lined both sides of the street. Struggling for breath, she slid off her bike and walked along the sidewalk to Victoria Park in the center of town.

In the shade of a towering tree, Maddy dropped her bike on the grass next to a concrete bench and sank into its cool seat. Shopping could wait. She pulled her puffer out of her pocket and inhaled from its spout. She closed her eyes and waited until her heart stopped racing. But ripples of emotion continued to roll over her—worry, fear, even excitement. But mostly she felt confusion. Had she really gone back in time? Was that old woman warning her about some strange disease lurking in her house? Or did octagons, like Poppa George said, let bad air flow through them and sweep germs right out the door? Could it get rid of her asthma? Or would all its strangeness make it worse?

A car honked. Maddy's eyes flew open. She gazed around her. Close by the bench, water splashed down the tiers of a round fountain. A breeze blew its cool spray onto her bare arms. She tried to rub the shivers out of them. In the bright sun on the other side of the road, stood a large brick building. Its sign said *Town Hall and Public Library* in bold black letters. A sandwich board on the sidewalk announced, *Library Open. Internet Available.*

Maddy wheeled her bike across the street and parked it in the rack. She let the sunshine warm her arms before she climbed the cement stairs towards the double oak doors. The light was dim inside the foyer of the building. A display of tourism brochures lined the wall in front of her. To the left an engraved, metal sign on the door read *Municipal Office*. On the right, an identical sign on an identical door said *Library*. Maddy turned its brass knob and pushed it open.

Behind the library's check-out desk, a young woman greeted her with a bright smile. "Can I help you?"

Maddy said, "I . . . I . . . want to use the computer."

The woman slid a clipboard towards her. "Here's the sign-up sheet. You're in luck. It's quiet today. Usually you have to wait an hour."

Maddy eased into a chair at one of the computer stations and for a minute stared at the monitor, her mind as blank as the screen. What did she want? She slowly moved the mouse around and logged onto Internet Explorer. What was the name of that coughing disease? Con . . . su . . . tion? After a few tries in Google, the word *consumption* appeared, and she clicked on Wikipedia. What she found did little to relieve her anxiety.

Tuberculosis, often called consumption before 1950, is a common and often lethal disease caused by Mycobacterium tuberculosis. It spreads through the air with a cough or sneeze, attacking the lungs and sometimes other parts of the body. Its symptoms are chronic coughing with blood-tinged sputum, fever, night sweats, and weight loss. Treatment is difficult and requires long courses of antibiotics. If left untreated, it kills more than 50 percent of those infected.

Maddy's head whirled. Chronic cough? Yes. Night sweats? Fever? Sometimes but not lately. Weight loss? Maybe. What's sputum? Blood-tinged sputum?

"Find what you're looking for? The library's closing in ten minutes," the cheerful librarian announced behind her.

Maddy groaned. She quickly skimmed over another site that described how antibiotics cured tuberculosis and then clicked on her email box to look for a message from Amy, hoping that maybe Amy's mother had agreed to drive her to Colebrook for a visit. Or better yet, had suggested that Maddy come to their cottage for a few weeks. Then she could escape her weird house. But, to Maddy's disappointment, the email inbox was empty. At that moment, the library lights flickered off. No time to ask Amy for an invite. She'd have to beg Dan for time on his computer after supper . . . if he didn't hog it the whole night.

With a few clicks of the mouse, Maddy reluctantly closed the computer screen. Outside, as she pulled her bike out of the rack, the jingle of coins in her pocket reminded her to stop at the supermarket. A half hour later she wearily pedaled home. When she turned in the driveway, she glimpsed a black shadow scurry under a lilac tree. She braked but then rolled the bike towards the garage. Too many troubling thoughts crowded her mind. She did not want to follow the cat into the woodshed and up the ladder.

Chapter 7

The sharp whistle of a cardinal woke Maddy the next morning. With each piercing chirp she remembered a scene from the day before—the attic room, the people below in the old kitchen, the click of Aunt Ella's knitting needles, the word *consumption* glaring at her from the computer screen, Dan's reluctant "okay" when she politely asked for time on his computer to email Amy.

"Five minutes, Maddy. I've got important work tonight," he had grumbled.

To which Maddy had groaned inwardly. Couldn't he spare it for once?

Thank goodness he had left early that morning. She slipped out of bed and tiptoed down to the den to check for a reply from Amy, but her inbox was still empty.

Maddy pressed her hands to the sides of her head and tried to send a telepathic message to the airwaves up north—*Wake up, Amy! Get me out of here!* Why did her

39

friend have to leave for her cottage so soon? She might never see her again.

Outside the window, the cardinal whistled twice. Maddy glanced up. Meters away, the black cat crouched under the maple tree in the front yard.

Maddy leaned back in Dan's chair and crossed her arms. "No way. I'm not following you." She scowled. "No matter how long you stick around." The cat looked up and meowed. Maddy closed her eyes and plugged her ears.

"Madison Rose!" a muffled voice shouted behind her. Maddy swung around in the chair. Her mother stood in the doorway, a puzzled look wrinkling her forehead. "Didn't you hear me? It's time to get dressed! We have doctors' appointments at ten o'clock this morning! Chop, chop!"

Maddy's stomach tightened. A doctor's appointment? Now? Would Dr. Wyatt discover something dreadfully wrong with her? Would she agree with that old woman? Would she say she had consumption and might cough blood and maybe even die? A feeling of doom settled inside Maddy, like dread before a math test she was certain she'd fail.

Two hours later, Maddy's feet dangled off the side of an examination table.

"Take a deep breath," Dr. Wyatt said as she tapped up and down Maddy's back. Then she shone a light in Maddy's eyes and ears and looked down her throat with quick efficiency.

"You've gained weight, Maddy! Congratulations!" The doctor beamed. "And your cheeks have color! Country life must suit you. Any questions?"

Maddy blinked, not sure she had heard the doctor

correctly. She shifted on the white paper covering the table. It crinkled underneath her legs.

"Uh, what's sputum?"

Dr. Wyatt's eyebrows rose a notch over her glasses. "It's mucous, Maddy. Coughed up from your lungs. Remember you did that when you had bronchitis? But that's over now, isn't it?"

Maddy shrugged. Was it? She stared at her bare feet. If she thought about it, she really hadn't coughed that hard in months. Nor did she have a fever, at least not here in the doctor's office. Apparently, she had even gained weight. The suffocating heaviness began to lift off Maddy's shoulders. If anything was dreadfully wrong, she concluded, the doctor wouldn't be smiling.

"How's your asthma? Need another refill for your puffer?" Dr. Wyatt asked. Maddy shook her head. She hadn't used it much lately. Only yesterday after her weird time in the attic and her bicycle trip into town.

"Good," Dr. Wyatt replied. "Just give me a call if you need another inhaler. In the meantime, stay active and get lots of sunshine. Rest when you're tired. You'll need extra energy to help your mother with the new addition to your family." She beamed at Carla whose hands lay on her protruding stomach.

"How are things with you?"

"A bit better. I just saw the obstetrician." Carla patted her stomach. "She advises me to take it easy for the next two months."

"Things finally settling down?" The doctor glanced at Maddy and then back at Carla, who quickly nodded in reply and looked away while she twisted the ring on her finger.

"Well, good luck with everything."

As they rode the elevator in silence, Maddy's mother leaned against the wall. Her eyes were closed. Her face was pale. When they reached the parking lot, she unlocked the car, slowly lowered herself into the driver's seat, and exhaled a long, weary sigh.

Maddy climbed in next to her and clicked the seatbelt into place.

"Is something wrong, Mom?"

For a moment Carla was silent. Then she smiled. "No, Maddy. Everything's fine. I'm just tired."

"Yeah, like all the time. Is that why your doctor wants you to take it easy?"

"Sort of." Her mother rubbed her forehead. "You see, I'm older now, Maddy. And even though I wanted another child, this one snuck up on me. It was a real surprise for Dan too. He never imagined us getting pregnant so soon. And then, well . . . I bled so much. . . ."

Maddy clapped her hands over her ears. "Whoa, too much information, Mom!"

Carla laughed. "Okay, but don't worry, Maddy. Everything's fine." She lightly caressed Maddy's cheek before twisting the key in the ignition. When she pulled onto the highway, she turned the radio off and said, "I know it's been hard moving to a new place where you don't know anyone, Maddy. So . . . maybe you'd like to visit Amy for a week or two?"

"Really! Go to her cottage?" Maddy could scarcely believe her ears. "How would I get there?"

"Dan said he could drive you."

"No way! I'm not sitting in a truck with him for hours

and hours!" Maddy frowned. "He'll just play that crappy country music and sing along. And eat granola bars and let the crumbs fall all over him!"

"Don't be rude, Maddy. You know he'd love to drive you there. You've got to spend time with him, get to know him better."

"He's always working! And when he's home, he doesn't pay any attention to me. He's always on his precious computer and he won't ever let me use it."

"That iMac cost Dan a lot of money and he needs it for business."

"Yeah, whatever." Maddy sniffed. She stared out the window before she burst out. "You know, Mom, I have a real dad. Somewhere."

Silence filled the car for a very long mile before Carla answered in a voice so quiet that Maddy strained to hear it.

"Yes, somewhere, Maddy. It's unfortunate that he's not into being a father or even getting in touch with you. I imagine he's rather wrapped up in his own life." She waited a moment and added. "Perhaps it's time to give Dan a chance. He'd be a good father."

"No way," Maddy exclaimed. "I'd rather find my own dad."

After another long pause, Carla answered. "I have no idea where your dad lives, Maddy. And right now, I'm simply too tired to find out. Besides, I'd just as soon not know what he's up to."

"Yeah, that's the problem. You're always too tired." Maddy snorted as she twisted away and sat stone-faced staring out the window, ignoring her mother's reach for a tissue from the box between them.

43

When they pulled into their driveway, Carla quietly gathered her purse and slipped out of the car, promising roast chicken and new potatoes from the garden for supper. But Maddy bolted to her room and firmly shut the door behind her. From under the bed, she pulled out a shoebox covered in white paper with the words *Private Box* and *Keep Out* written in purple bubble letters on the lid. Flowers and doodles of every color danced across it. Inside were her treasures . . . old coins and a two-dollar Dominion of Canada bill from Poppa George, Grammy Bea's onyx ring, and cards from her father. There were four birthday cards decorated with balloons and glittery words and underneath them, two postcards that sported koala bears and crocodiles with short messages of *wish you were here* scrawled on their backs.

At the bottom of the box lay a framed photograph. In it, a young man with bushy, red hair held a baby in his arms, one hand around its middle, while the other waved the baby's hand at the camera. Maddy picked it up and traced her finger over the man's face. He grinned back at her, reflecting her own face with its green eyes and a smattering of freckles across the nose.

"Where are you?" she whispered. She wondered what it would be like to drive with him to Amy's cottage. For sure, he'd let her play her own music. And stop for ice cream on the way. It didn't matter that he had disappeared to Australia so long ago that she barely had any memories of him. If he came back now, he'd still be her father. Even if Dan was on the scene. Why wouldn't her mother try to find him? Everybody needed a real father. Not a pretend one.

"I'm going to put your picture on the wall downstairs,"

she told the man in the photo. "And take down their stupid wedding picture." Just the thought of that photograph taken in front of City Hall made her angry. Dan had no right barging into their lives and taking up all her mother's attention. It had been a snowy day in March when her mother and Dan were married. Everyone in the photo looked happy—Mom, Dan the Man, Poppa George, a few friends. Even the skaters in the background circling round and round the rink. But not Maddy. She had shivered the whole time the photographer's camera clicked away. She looked frozen in place, standing ever-so-slightly away from the smiling wedding party.

Holding her father's picture, Maddy sank into her bed. Exhausted, she fell into a light sleep. She dreamed that she climbed the ladder to the loft in the woodshed. When she opened the trunk, there was a photo of her father leaning out a car window. "Get in, Maddy!" he called. She struggled to reach him and rolled off the bed. Startled awake, she clambered to her feet.

Had her father really called her? Did the trunk in the attic hold a clue to his whereabouts? She listened for voices but heard only water pipes rattle in the bathroom below. She stumbled down the stairs. The air in the woodshed was cool as Maddy climbed to the loft. She felt relief when she didn't see the outline of a door in the back wall. Dropping to her knees, she pushed up the trunk lid. From the folds of the quilt, the black cat with its white-tipped tail stared impassively at her. Maddy tugged the quilt out and jabbed her fingers into the corners of the trunk. There was no photograph of her father anywhere in it.

"I don't get it," she cried, bitter disappointment welling

up inside her. "In my dream, his picture was right here in this trunk. I heard him calling my name."

She wiped her eye on the quilt and pushed it back into the trunk, not caring if the cloth cat sat on top. Not caring if the doll with the sweet face tumbled to the bottom. It was so hard to sort out her feelings about her father and Dan. She scarcely remembered the one who had left her long ago. The other was an annoying, daily presence. She didn't know what to do about either of them.

Maddy sat with her arms wrapped tightly around her knees and listened to the goldfinch twittering in the garden. After a while, her shoulders relaxed and she let her mind drift until a tickle of fur brushed against her arm. She jerked around in time to see a white-tipped tail disappear through the small door at the back of the loft. But Maddy didn't budge. She stared at the opening. She really didn't want to trek back into the past. It was stranger than the present. Then the whiskered face reappeared in the doorway and cocked its head.

"You think I should just get up and follow you?" she scowled.

The cat sat, ears straight up, and gazed at her. With a meow, it stood, flicked its tail, and disappeared into the attic, as if to say, *It's up to you.*

"All right then." Maddy pushed the trunk lid closed. "I will."

Chapter 8

A hot afternoon sun streamed through the attic window. The air was stifling. Maddy hurried across the floor and down the steep stairs into the creamery below where no milk cooled in the tank and no sounds came from the room beyond. She peeked into the kitchen. No one. Instead, a white-tipped tail beckoned her like a finger to follow it out the back door.

Hesitantly she stepped outside. To her left, she saw a familiar door, its boards now straight and unpainted. Attached to the woodshed was a rough, open outbuilding sheltering a black buggy inside its walls. On her right, an iron pump stood like a sentinel, its metal arm pointing towards an enormous red barn that loomed beyond the dirt driveway. There, a tall boy wearing a cap led a horse into the barn's dark interior. Behind them marched the black cat.

Heart thumping, Maddy crossed the rutted driveway

and skirted the chicken run where yellow hens scratched in the dirt. Inside the barn, the air was cool. Dust danced in the sunlight that streaked between the barn boards. The sweet smell of fresh-cut hay filled the air. Maddy spotted the boy tethering his horse in a stall near a cobweb-coated window. He scarcely looked up when she blocked the light from the door.

"Aunt Ella's in the house if you've come for eggs," he muttered reaching for a currycomb.

"I'm not here for eggs."

"You the new boy at Franklin's store?"

"Nooo."

"If you're not here for eggs, what brings you?" His voice was as chilly as the barn, not at all friendly.

Out of the corner of her eye, Maddy glimpsed a blur of fur scooting behind a feed bag.

"I think that black cat has something to do with it."

"Shadow?" The boy snorted as he brushed the horse's neck. "She's just an ole black cat."

Maddy rubbed her hands on her jeans. "I'm not sure about that. She hangs around your Aunt Ella who's kinda spooky, sitting in her chair all hunched over, talking 'bout seeing me in her dreams."

The boy whirled around. His eyes widened. "You're a girl!" Then his face darkened in a frown. "But you ain't dressed like one. Who are you?"

"Maddy." She gulped.

"Where did you come from? You don't live 'round here."

Maddy shifted from one foot to another, debating what to explain to this prickly boy. After a moment, he raised his eyebrows as if to say *Well?* Maddy took a deep breath.

"Actually, I just moved here. Into that house." She waved her hand towards the driveway. "'Cept it's in the future. Your future, not mine. And don't ask me to explain, 'cause I have no idea how I go back in time . . . but I do . . . when that black cat appears out of nowhere." Maddy's voice dropped to a whisper. "It was meowing at me today . . . though I heard a voice . . . my dad's . . . or maybe it was a dream. Maybe you're a dream too."

The boy's mouth opened and closed. Then he shrugged. "You sound a bit daft! And you look strange . . . wearing pants like a boy."

"You look strange too," Maddy retorted. "Boys in my time wouldn't be caught dead in short pants and long socks."

The boy turned stiffly away, picked up a wide-tooth comb, and pulled it through the horse's tail with long strokes. Afraid she had offended him, Maddy said in a rush, "I just moved here. I used to live in the city, but my stepfather Dan dragged us out here right after he married my mom."

The boy did not reply. He placed the comb on a shelf and scooped oats into a pail for the horse. Maddy watched him for a moment and then, with a shrug, turned to leave.

"I have no idea what you're talking about. Maybe you're lost," said the boy, as he dumped the grain into the horse's feed trough. "But don't go, I don't mind if you visit for a bit." He set down the pail and stepped forward, hand outstretched. "Name's Clarence. But most folks call me Clare."

Surprised by his sudden, friendly gesture, Maddy hesitated a second. Then she wiped her palms on her jeans and shook his hand. His skin felt rough, but his fingers strong. She smiled shyly.

Clare looked down at his feet. "I live here with my Uncle Ray and Aunt Helen. And my great-aunt, Ella. Been doing so for nigh two years."

At first, Maddy didn't know what to say, but then she blurted, "Where are your parents?"

"Mother lives with my sister Eva in a boarding house in Belleville. She works in a milliner's shop making fancy hats for ladies. She don't make enough money to look after me too."

"Well, what about your dad?" Maddy pressed on, surprised at her boldness. She hoped he didn't mind her questions.

Clare picked up a broom and, with short swipes, pushed the loose straw into a pile.

"Don't know."

Don't know? Did his father disappear too? If so, Maddy guessed that Clare probably wouldn't tell her any more. Some things weren't easy to talk about. Especially absent fathers.

"Yeah," she said. "Mine's gone too. Disappeared when I was a little kid. Someday I'm going to find out where he lives. Maybe even move in with him."

Clare raised his eyes, stared at her for a moment, and then continued sweeping the floor. With her foot, Maddy shoved bits of straw towards his pile. Its dust tickled her nose and she sneezed over and over, in sharp, staccato bursts. Clare backed away.

"No worries. I'm just allergic to dust," Maddy said. "For sure, I don't have that coughing disease like . . . uh, like your sister."

"How'd you know about Eva?" The boy's expression

darkened.

Maddy didn't want to admit she'd been watching them through the grate in the attic floor.

"Umm, like I told you . . . your Aunt Ella. She said your sister's always tired. And she coughs a lot." Her voice dropped. "She's pretty sick, eh?"

Clare winced and turned away.

"Sorry."

Maddy ran her hand through her hair. Had she offended him again? Maybe she should leave him alone. But the sadness in the droop of his shoulders resonated with her own loneliness. She felt an unexpected connection to him.

"I don't mean to upset you. It's just that I was sick all last winter. Coughing and always tired. Still am. And I get asthma sometimes. So your aunt weirded me out. Made me think I had consumption too. Like Eva."

For a moment, Clare continued to stare out the window. Then he leaned against the stall boards. "Last time I seen her, she didn't seem so sick. But now she's getting weaker." His chin quivered ever so slightly. "I just wish I could do something."

"Well, doesn't she take antibiotics?"

"Take what?"

"Antibiotics. Medicine. Didn't her doctor give her any pills?"

Clare stared at Maddy. "There you go again! I got no idea what you're talking about. The doctor said she needs rest and fresh air. Well, she gets lots of that when she stays here. But it ain't helping her. And all those bottles of smelly cod liver oil, they ain't helping either. She just gags and gags when she tries to swallow it."

Clare stamped his foot and Maddy jumped. She didn't know what to say. She had never heard of cod liver oil. She was sure Wikipedia hadn't mentioned it.

A shout from the driveway broke the silence.

"It's Uncle Ray!" Clare dropped his broom. "I'll see what he wants."

Chapter 9

Uncertain what to do, Maddy shrank towards the back of the barn where tools hung on dusty barn boards. When a cobweb brushed her cheek, she batted it away furiously and wished she had followed Clare into the open air. But before she could make up her mind, an exasperated voice hollered from the driveway.

"Dang it, Clare, there's a boulder in the field needs diggin' out and I need your help."

"I'll get the pickaxe and be right there, Uncle Ray!"

Clare rushed back into the barn, almost smack into Maddy standing in the shadows.

"Best be gone," he said rather sternly after he regained his balance. "I'll be helping Uncle Ray for some time. He ain't partial to strangers." He lifted a long-handled pickaxe off its nail. And then, without looking back, he strode out the door.

Maddy felt bewildered by his sudden disappearance and

wary of his uncle's unfriendliness. The dust in the barn began to tickle her throat. She waited until the voices faded away. Then she crept to the wide barn doors. No one was in sight. In a black blur, Shadow scooted past her and across the driveway. Maddy followed her into the house.

There was no one in the kitchen, nor in the creamery. Even the cat had vanished. Not knowing what else to do, Maddy opened the green door that led to the attic. Maybe she should wait up there till Clare returned. At the top step, she paused. The light in the long room seemed hazy, the jumbled furniture indistinct. Everything was utterly silent. She turned towards the wall where the small door led into the woodshed loft. Its outline wavered and began to disappear as if an invisible hand were erasing it off a blackboard. From below, she heard a faint voice.

"Maddy, where are you?"

She stepped quickly towards the wall and reached for the iron latch just before it faded away. With a sharp jerk, she pulled the door open and ducked into the woodshed loft of her own time.

"Maddy!" the voice called again. "Supper's ready!"

Maddy hesitated. She wasn't ready to leave the past, but when she turned around, the small door had vanished.

She gasped. "So weird! How does a door just disappear?"

Downstairs, her mother called again, a note of impatience in her voice.

Again Maddy hesitated, baffled by how suddenly one reality replaced another. But when she heard her mother's exasperated voice in the creamery below, Maddy climbed down the ladder, and slowly made her way out of the woodshed, across the back porch, and into her kitchen.

"Where were you?" Carla asked as she leaned forward to brush a cobweb out of Maddy's hair.

Without replying, Maddy twisted away and headed to the sink to wash her hands. During supper, she pushed the food around her plate. Images of Clare floated in and out of her mind. His scowl when he first saw her in the barn. The feel of his strong fingers shaking her hand. The pain in his eyes when she mentioned Eva's name.

As if she were sitting far away, Maddy heard her mother tell Dan about their visits to the doctors earlier in the day.

"The doctor says that everything looks good," Carla said, patting her stomach.

A slow smile lit Dan's face. He reached over and squeezed Carla's hand.

"What about you, Maddy?" he asked. "What did your doctor say?"

"Not much."

"Maddy, you have good news too. Tell Dan what she said."

"I'm fine. Just need fresh air and rest. Same old thing."

"That's good news, Maddy!" Dan flashed her a warm smile. "No more meds?"

Maddy shook her head. Meds. Antibiotics. That's what she needed to do! Find them for Eva. She tried to remember where she had last seen the bottle of white oval pills. Most likely in the bathroom cupboard.

For the rest of supper, she listened restlessly to the conversation swirling around her. Dan described a new building project. Something about making old-fashioned trim for new houses. Just like the gingerbread pattern of some old brick mansion overlooking Lake Ontario a hundred years ago.

Dan turned to Maddy. "You'll be happy to hear, Maddy, that Martin, the new foreman on the job, has a daughter your age. They're a sailing family. They've bought a house in town and invited us to join them for supper one night on their sailboat moored at the marina."

"That's fantastic!" Carla beamed. "Sounds like moving out here was the right idea for everyone."

Maddy shrugged. Her mind was preoccupied with thoughts of Eva and her urge to find the antibiotics. She could barely focus on her mother's enthusiastic description of her latest photography assignment for *Country Crafts* magazine.

"It's about handmade soap. I can make it right here in our kitchen using lavender flowers from the garden. I'll take pictures of each step. The magazine sent me a book about the whole process."

"Whoa!" Dan exclaimed. "That's dangerous! You need lye to make soap. It's a nasty chemical. You shouldn't be working by a hot stove breathing those fumes when you're pregnant!"

Maddy stopped toying with her food. Was this an argument? Dan looked sterner than she had ever seen him. She shrank inside herself, away from the tension in the room. After a moment of silence, Carla patted her husband's hand.

"Honey, I plan to make the simple stuff with soap bars that I've already bought. All I have to do is add my own lavender flowers and some lavender oil. No lye. No danger. No worries!"

When Dan scowled again, Carla crossed her arms on top of her stomach and leaned back in her chair. She was quiet for a minute, but then she promised to wait until after the baby was born. Dan harrumphed and muttered that it still wasn't a good idea. Maddy stared at her hands, thinking he was acting like Dan the Man again. Her mother said nothing but stood and began to clear the table. After a moment, Dan picked up the remaining dishes and slid them into the dishwasher.

While Dan and Carla washed the pots and pans in silence, Maddy retreated to the bathroom and locked the door. She turned on the taps in the old-fashioned tub, hoping the sound of rushing water would mask her search for the antibiotics. In the medicine cabinet, she found bottles of aspirin and antacids, small jars of cream and nail polish, but no medicine bottle with the white oval pills inside. The towel cupboard held linens, suntan lotion, mosquito repellent, and on the bottom shelf, a dozen white bars of soap and a bottle of lavender oil, the ingredients for Carla's soap project.

"Guess they'll have to stay put for a while," Maddy said with a snort.

Then she remembered the vitamin bottles by the spices and herbs in the kitchen cupboard. She splashed the water in the tub, dampened a towel, and pulled the plug. For extra measure, she flushed the toilet. When she cracked open the bathroom door, she heard the television in the living room. The coast was clear. Maddy tiptoed to the kitchen cupboard. In the shadows of the deep shelf, she spotted a plastic bottle with her name on the label. She shoved it into her pocket.

Once in her bedroom, Maddy counted the pills. Twelve. Not many. But enough to get Eva started. Somehow, she had to get them to Clare. And, somehow, he had to get them to Eva. She crossed her fingers that Shadow would turn up in the morning and that the door would magically appear again.

*****

When the first light of dawn seeped through her bedroom window, Maddy shoved the curtain aside. The black cat sat licking herself in the grass where the barn once stood.

"Yes!" Maddy pumped her fist. "Let's find Clare!" She popped the lid of the pill bottle, dumped its contents into a small sock that she could easily tuck into her jean pocket and headed to the woodshed.

Like the day before, no one was in the old kitchen. Maddy heard the chime of a clock ringing in the octagon. She followed its silvery sound into the parlor. No one was there either. How different it looked from her own living room. Its ceiling was covered in grooved, gray boards. Dark, oak wainscoting ran around the angled, outside walls. Along an inside wall, a brick fireplace rose to the low ceiling. It was flanked by a prim, striped sofa and a sturdy chair with an embroidered seat. Maddy thought they didn't look very comfy, not like the cushy couch and recliner in her living room.

Through the far window, she glimpsed a horse and wagon bumping down the road. A wiry man in a straw hat held the reins. Next to him sat a young woman with a parasol, and between them, a small, hunched woman in black.

Everyone was leaving. Aunt Ella too. But where was Clare?

Maddy dashed outside to the barn. As she burst through its doors, a mound of straw landed at her feet. Bits of chaff floated up. She sneezed. A head peered through the square hole above her.

"Watch out! You won't like it if it lands on you."

"No kidding, Clare! You watch out. I'm coming up." Maddy scrambled to the hayloft.

"You look like a farmer!" She grinned at him. He was dressed in overalls and held a pitchfork in one hand. Small bits of straw stuck in his hair. "Where's everyone going today?"

"To town," he frowned. "It's a shopping day."

"Why are you still here?"

"Getting chores done. Watch where you're standing!"

Clare forked another pile of straw and swung around to pitch it below.

Maddy jumped aside. The air was thick with dust. She sneezed again and again. Rubbing her nose, she spotted an open window on the far side of the barn. When she leaned out for a breath of air, she saw a scene very different from the one she knew from her own time. There were hardly any trees around the house. To the west, field after field stretched all the way to the concession road.

Across the dirt road to the east, she saw a small field of high grass. A horse grazed by a rail fence. Further back, beyond an uneven line of cedar trees, water sparkled in a large pond. From it, a stream rushed towards a ramshackle building and tumbled over a creaking waterwheel behind it.

"What's that old building across the road?"

Clare stabbed his pitchfork into a mound of straw and joined her by the window. "That's the old mill. My great-grandpa built it for grinding corn an' wheat when they first cleared the land.

Now Uncle Ray makes soap there when he's not farm-ing."

Makes soap? Dan the Man's scowling face flashed before her. She turned to Clare, her eyes wide open.

"Can we go there, to the mill? I want to see how it's done."

"How what's done?"

"Making soap. I hear it's dangerous."

"It is. You can't go there. Uncle Ray don't like girls and womenfolk in the old mill. Them floors are slippery. You could take a tumble and get real hurt."

"You sound like my stepdad, Dan the Man! He's always fussing about dangerous things." Maddy frowned. "Don't worry! I'll be careful." She headed towards the ladder, but Clare blocked her way.

"Good thing you're wearing pants, even if you're a girl, but you need boots. Chemicals for making soap can burn you!"

"Well, got any?" Maddy demanded, ignoring his comment about her clothes. "All I have are my running shoes."

Clare nodded. "Down there. The ones Eva wears out riding."

Eva's boots? Maddy hesitated. Did they have germs? Should she wear them? But, afraid of offending Clare and very curious about the soap factory, she followed him down the ladder. When he held up a pair of boots, she took them and pulled them on, laced their leather ties, and followed Clare's silence into the sunlight and across the road to the mill.

Chapter 10

With a heave, Clare slid open the mill's wooden door. Maddy entered behind him into the cavernous space where only a dim light seeped through dirty windows high above their heads. After, the brightness of the sun, Maddy's eyes slowly widened at the cluttered scene before her. Then her nose twitched.

"Ewww. What's that smell?"

Something was rotting, something far worse than a garbage pail left too long under the kitchen sink.

"That's the beef fat boiling on the stove behind you. We use it to make the soap. Uncle Ray's collecting more from the butcher now."

Maddy stared at the enormous wood stove. From a large black pot, steam rose lazily into the air, spreading the rancid odor throughout the building.

"You make soap with that foul stuff?"

Clare picked up a log from a pile on the floor. He opened

the stove door and pitched it inside.

"You prob'ly buy Sunlight Soap, all wrapped in fancy papers," he said with a shake of his head. "City ladies love it. Even country women fancy it to our soap."

Maddy had never heard of Sunlight Soap. She shrugged and turned towards the large, dark room. Its disorder was unlike any she had ever seen. Small wooden barrels and rusty cans lay scattered here and there. In the middle of the huge space, stood an enormous, round tub. In the ceiling, a metal rod extended from the back wall and hung directly over the tub, dropping a paddle the size of a large oar into the center. A three-legged iron vat with a spigot at its bottom leaned towards the tub. Maddy eyed it uneasily.

"That looks like a witch's cauldron."

"Don't touch it! There's lye in it."

Maddy shrank back and bumped into Clare. He grasped her arm to steady her.

"I told you. This place ain't for girls! It's dangerous."

Exasperation prickled Maddy. She yanked her arm back.

"What's so dangerous about making soap?"

"Lye can burn you real good. Uncle Ray wears leather gloves and goggles when he's using it."

Maddy lifted her chin. "Don't worry so much. I'm not stupid. I won't touch it." She tilted her head in challenge. "So tell me, what do you do with that lye stuff?"

Clare's lips tightened for a moment, but then his shoulders began to relax. "Making soap's complicated," he said with resignation. "See those cans of soda ash on the floor? Well, you mix water with that stuff in this here vat, the one you called a witch's cauldron, and you let it sit awhile, till it turns to lye. Like I said, it's nasty stuff. Burns your skin. Blinds you if a drop gets in your eye. And it's got nasty fumes too. Real bad for your nose."

"I'm surprised your uncle lets you in here," she smirked, thinking his dramatic description of the process made the mill seem like a deathtrap for *anyone* who walked through its doors.

Clare snorted, but continued. "Then Uncle Ray siphons the lye out of the vat using this here hose." With a boot, he nudged the greasy hose attached to the spigot. It snaked away from the vat towards the wooden tub. "He mixes the lye with tallow in that tub."

"What's tallow?"

"The beef fat you smell cooking on the stove."

With a sidelong glance at Clare, Maddy skirted far around the iron vat to the huge tub. She peered over its edge. A thin greasy scum coated its bottom.

"It's empty!"

"Yeah, like I said, we're making tallow now. On the stove!" A note of impatience crept into Clare's voice. "Later, when it's all melted, Uncle Ray'll dump it in the tub and add the lye."

He waved his hand at the high ceiling. "See that metal rod 'tached to the paddle above the tub? It's connected to the water wheel outside. So when the wheel turns, the paddle mixes everything up. After a while, a chem'cal reaction turns it to soap. Don't know myself how it happens. But it does. Takes an hour or two."

Maddy stared into the tub. "What do you do with the stuff after that?"

Clare pointed to a pail with a long handle hanging on a pillar.

"We use buckets to scoop the soft soap out of the tub. Then we pour it into molds." He pointed to the long, shallow stands on the other side of the tub. "There's a batch of soap in 'em now."

Maddy carefully stepped up to one of the stands and ran a finger along its smooth edge. Then she touched the shiny expanse of soap.

"It's like a miniature ice rink."

"Soap's been hard'ning for a couple of days. When it's cured, Uncle Ray'll cut it into bars. Then I'll press it."

Clare picked up a bar of the yellow soap and inserted it into a small, metal machine. When he pushed its handle, a round stamp pounded into the soap. He slid the bar out of the press and handed it to Maddy. She traced the scripted 'S' on its surface and held it to her nose. It didn't smell like the horrid tallow on the wood stove. In fact, it hardly smelled at all.

"Is the S for Sanders?"

Clare nodded.

"Can I keep it?"

"Sure. We got lots." Clare waved his hand towards the rows of soap on shelves under the windows.

"This afternoon I'll pack some into crates, and tomorrow I'll bring 'em to stores in town . . . the ones that still take 'em. Nowadays the merchants only want that Sunlight Soap. Ours is cheaper, but soda ash is getting 'spensive. Pretty soon we won't be able to afford—" He cocked his ear towards the open door. "A wagon's coming up the road!" Clare said, running his hand through his hair. "Uncle Ray won't be pleased to see ya here. Best stay out back till he's gone."

Maddy hurried through a narrow side door and crouched in the tall grass next to the mill. She watched Clare and the older man roll large wooden barrels up a ramp into the building. Uncle Ray's face was covered with a stubbly dark beard. He, too, wore overalls, and a patched cotton shirt spotted with grease stains, its rolled sleeves revealing the thin ropey muscles of his arms. When he finally climbed back into the wagon and drove away, Clare poked his head out the door and motioned for Maddy.

"He's comin' back soon with more barrels. You can't stay here no more."

Maddy agreed. She didn't want to meet his Uncle Ray any more than he wanted her in the mill.

"Okay, bye," she whispered and flashed a quick smile at Clare before hastening out the mill's wide entrance and across the road to the house. As she opened its kitchen door, a soft voice called from the parlor.

"Clare," she heard Aunt Helen say. "Mrs. Franklin at the store needs eggs for baking."

Maddy darted into the creamery and up the stairs to the attic. But when she reached the wall, the outline of the door into the woodshed had vanished.

Chapter 11

M addy dropped the bar of soap and fell to her knees. She jabbed at the rough boards. No door swung open. She banged the wall with her fist. Nothing budged. It was as solid as concrete. Bubbles of panic rose inside her. Where was the cat? It always showed up when the door was open. She searched frantically around the room. But it wasn't under the bed or the dresser. Nor was it in the shadowy corners. In fact, it wasn't anywhere in the attic.

Maddy scrambled to her feet and paced back and forth. Each time she passed the place where the door had been, she gave the wall a kick. But it didn't budge. Soon the attic's stifling summer air closed around her. Sweat trickled down her cheeks. Her throat started to tighten. With a frantic tug, she slid the window open. A breeze cooled her face. Why had she been in such a rush that she forgot to take her puffer with her?

Maddy   collapsed   onto   the   bed   and   stared

despondently around the room. In a dark corner, the wooden rocking horse stared back at her with its hollow black eyes. She shivered and curled into a ball on the mattress. Slowly the light began to fade. Below, a knife chopped methodically on a cutting board. A pot clanged on the stove. Soon the smell of boiling potatoes drifted through the metal grate on the far side of the room.

Was her mother also cooking supper? Did she miss her yet? Maddy had been gone for hours, but she suspected that time between past and present did not match up. Maybe no one even noticed she had left her bedroom. Maybe they wouldn't discover her absence until much later in their day. And then what would they do? There was no way they could find her. She was stuck in the past. Alternating waves of fear and helplessness washed over her. A heavy weight settled on her chest, causing her breath to catch in her throat. She wanted to scream for help. But that would only freak out Clare's family. Instead, to calm herself, she tried to breathe slowly, in and out, like the doctor had taught her. Then she focused on the noises below—chairs scraping over the floor, forks clinking against plates, the rise and fall of voices. When these sounds faded away, Maddy's breath had evened out and she drifted into a light sleep.

The room was dark when she awoke. The space around her seemed cavernous. Where was she? In the moonlight shining through the window, Maddy recognized the outlines of a broken chair and a washstand. Memories of the day rushed back. She pushed herself up, listening for sounds below, but all was quiet. Everyone was sleeping. When her stomach rumbled with a gnawing hunger, she crept downstairs in search of food.

After a glance around the dark kitchen, Maddy slipped into the pantry. Gray shadows filled the little room. Under a small window, moonlight shone on the hand pump next to a metal sink. Above it, dishes hunched on a rack. Where, Maddy wondered as her stomach growled louder, did they store their food?

In the moonlight, she spotted a wooden box with a handle. When she tugged it, a door swung open and cool air brushed her cheek. A refrigerator? Maddy's fingers groped inside until they touched a tall, glass bottle. Ah, milk! She poured a mug and gulped it down. Still hungry, she searched for something to eat.

On the table next to the wooden box lay a loaf of bread covered with a cloth napkin. Maddy broke off a chunk and stuffed it in her mouth. She tore off a larger piece and slipped back upstairs. As she sat on the bed slowly chewing each morsel, she realized that she hadn't seen the cat downstairs. Had it snuck up to the attic when she left the green door ajar? As she bent to look for it under the bed, the small sock dropped from her pocket onto the floor.

The pills! She had totally forgotten to give the pills to Clare. Maddy picked up the sock and rolled the pills over and over with her fingers. A worrisome thought skittered into her mind. Had Shadow stayed away because she hadn't given the pills to Clare? She had been so distracted by the soap factory that maybe it was her fault the portal wouldn't open. She had better stay put until morning and then find Clare. Yawning, she untied Eva's boots and slowly sank back onto the bed.

*****

Hours later, faint footsteps below woke Maddy from a

dreamless sleep. Groggily, she sat up and stared at the wall in the morning light. Still no outline of a door. From downstairs, the wood stove door banged closed. The stove pipe rattled as warm air rose through it and out the chimney. Taking a deep breath, Maddy cautiously edged towards the grate in the floor and glimpsed Clare's tousled head below her.

"Clare," she hissed. "I'm stuck up in the attic!"

In seconds, he had scrambled up the stairs and poked his head through the trap door. "Why are you here? I thought you left yesterday."

"I can't go home! The door to the woodshed disappeared!"

When Clare raised his finger to his lips, Maddy whispered, "Shadow's missing. When she's here, the door's here! But I haven't seen her in ages and now I can't go home."

Clare shook his head in disbelief. "No cat makes doors appear and disappear." He glanced at the wall and then at her. "Well, no matter, you can come with me t'day. I got soap deliveries to make."

Maddy glanced at him sideways. And a pill delivery too, if she could convince him that they would cure Eva. She pointed to her jeans and T-shirt. "Can I go with you dressed like this?"

Clare waved his hand at the wall. "There's one of Eva's old dresses on the hook. Hurry. I'll meet you in the barn." Without another word, he disappeared down the stairs.

Maddy tugged the striped, cotton dress over her head. The skirt fell below her knees. Should she button the sleeves at her wrists? Or roll them up? Already the air in the attic was warming rapidly. With unpracticed fingers, she wrapped the sash around her waist and tied an uneven bow. Next, she tucked the blue sock deep in the skirt's side pocket. As soon as possible, she would show the pills to Clare. She lifted the straw hat from its hook with a flourish, tied its ribbon under her chin, and retrieved the boots she had kicked off the night before. Quiet as the cat, she descended the stairs to the room below. By the time she reached the barn, Clare had hooked the horse up to the wagon.

He surveyed her transformation in silence as she climbed onto the seat next to him. Behind her, in the wagon bed, rested a dozen crates with *Sanders Soap* lettered on their sides. A small leather bag perched on the nearest one.

"There's bread and cheese if you're hungry."

"I'm starving! Thanks!"

With a jolt that nearly bumped Maddy off her seat, the horse pulled the wagon onto the dirt road. The mill was dark when they passed it. Maddy bit into a chunk of cheese and tore a large piece of bread off the loaf. As she ate, the wagon rattled along the road in and out of the shade of large, sugar maples. When the wagon gained speed, its wheels stirred up little swirls of dust. Maddy sneezed and wiped her nose with her sleeve. With the early morning sun warm on her face, she gazed around at the half dozen houses spaced far apart by vegetable gardens. Behind each squatted a small square barn. The scene was so different from the crowd of bungalows lining the street in her own time. Only a brick house here and there seemed familiar, and the creek at the bend in the road.

When they stopped at the intersection, Clare turned the horse and wagon west onto the main street leading into town. A cluster of buildings crowded the corners of the two dirt roads—a sprawling, white house, a small furniture store, and the East Colebrook General Store. Clare stopped the wagon in front of the latter.

Hopping down, he commanded, "Stay here. I gotta make a delivery." He leaned over the wagon and selected a crate. Even though the sign in the window said *closed*, the front door swung open when Clare mounted the steps.

Curious eyes swept over Maddy. A plump woman wrapped in a crisp, white apron bent down for the crate.

"Thanks, young man. We ain't sold all yer soap yet, but I'll take more in hopes sales pick up real soon." She slid the crate onto the step.

"Did you bring my eggs?"

Clare reached under the seat for a small wooden box with a wire handle. Mrs. Franklin leaned forward, took the box, and dropped two coins into his hand. He mumbled "Thanks, ma'am" and climbed back into the wagon.

"Nice ya have some comp'ny t'day. Stop by on yer way home. I'll be makin' peach ice cream." As she watched them pull back onto the road, Maddy leaned towards Clare.

"That sounds delicious, Clare."

"Won't be no money for ice cream."

"She just gave you some! It's in your pocket."

"Aunt Helen 'spects it."

"All of it? Doesn't your aunt or uncle pay you for your work?"

"Nope."

"Really? Don't you get an allowance?"

"A what?"

"An allowance. You know, the money you get every week

for doing chores. So you can buy your own things."

Clare snorted. "Never heard of it. I just do my chores like everyone else. Don't expect wages. Uncle Ray says soon I'll be old enough t' pay them room 'n board."

Now Maddy was puzzled. "What's that?"

"Money you pay for meals and lodging."

"Lodging? Like your bedroom? You'll have to pay to sleep in your own house?"

"Course I will. After I finish school."

Clare explained that all his farm friends paid room and board if they worked in the orchards or for a farmer. "Just the way it is," he stated. "When I get a job, I give my earnings to Aunt Ella."

"Well, how do you buy clothes? And other stuff?"

"Aunt Ella sews our clothes. Don't need much else."

Maddy sank back onto the wagon seat. It was too awkward asking questions about wages or room and board. After all, she hardly did any chores to earn her allowance each week. And she spent it on whatever she chose—candy, pop, CDs, movies. She never paid for her own clothes or food, certainly not to sleep in her own bed. She couldn't imagine not having money to buy ice cream or pop if she wanted them.

Maddy retreated into silence as the horse trotted towards town, first past the furniture store and then the brick church. In a long expanse of field, she watched swallows swoop over rows of cut hay drying in the early morning sun. When the low whistle of a train moaned in the distance, she glanced sideways at Clare. He was staring straight ahead. His face had lost its grim expression. With a small flourish, she pulled the sock out of her pocket and presented it to him.

Chapter 12

Clare looked at the sock in Maddy's upturned hand. "What's that?"

"Pills for Eva!" She untied the sock, poured out a few, and showed them to him.

"They ain't going to help her," he said flicking the reins. As the horse picked up its pace, Maddy instinctively curled her fingers around the pills.

"Why not? They cured me when I was coughing up a storm last winter."

"'Cause she ain't here to take 'em."

"No kidding, Clare!" Maddy eyed him. For the first time she noticed his thick eyelashes. They almost veiled his eyes. He was kinda cute, she realized and then quickly looked away. She took a deep breath, hoping her face hadn't reddened and her voice sounded normal.

"Can't you take them to her?"

Clare flicked the reins again. A milk wagon rattled by.

The driver tipped his hat and Clare nodded in return.

"Like I told you," he finally said avoiding her eyes. "Eva lives far away in Belleville. I ain't got money for train tickets. 'Sides, Mother's taking her to the States for the Cure."

"The Cure?"

"People with the Cough go to a hospital in the mountains where they get lots of fresh air and more rest then you can imagine. They sit outside in the cold for hours." Clare shook his head in disbelief.

"Really? Outside in the cold?" When Maddy had bronchitis, her doctor ordered her to stay indoors, to not get chilled, no matter what. "That's crazy! Do they get better?"

"Some do. Some don't. Depends."

"On what?"

"Don't really know, although lots of people go there. They stay in hotels and some people even rent rooms in people's houses. Every day, the Coughers . . . that's what they call the folks who get sick . . . get dressed real warm and sit outside for hours in lounge chairs on big verandas. If they feel better, they get up and go for long walks. They have to eat all their meals, every last mouthful, even if they don't feel hungry. If they got lots of money, some stay there for years and get better. Some folks just get sicker and cough until they die."

"That's pretty grim! Don't they take any medicine, like antibiotics?" Maddy asked incredulously, thrusting her hand out.

"You mean those pills?" Clare shrugged. "Don't think the doctor mentioned 'em."

With an exasperated sigh, Maddy shoved the pills back into the sock. After a moment, Clare pointed to them with his elbow. "You think they'd help her?"

"You bet I do!" Maddy turned towards him so fast that the sock slipped onto the floorboards. As she bent down to retrieve it, Clare tugged on the reins and slowed the horse.

"Best sit still!" He grinned at her as she regained her balance.

"All you have to do is buy a train ticket and bring them to her." Maddy straightened her straw hat. "That's a lot easier than Eva traveling all that ways for that cure thing."

"Maybe," Clare said with a faraway look in his eyes. "I sure do miss her. She's my only sister, and if . . ." His voice trailed away as he focused on the road ahead, lost in his own thoughts.

For a while, they bumped along in silence. What would Eva do in the mountains, Maddy wondered. Sit on a cold porch for hours? Read books? Talk to herself? Last winter, when Maddy had been sick for days on end, she had grown very bored. But she'd been able to load the VCR with her favorite movies or play games on the computer. Poor Eva. She'd go crazy. And what would Clare do if she never stopped coughing and he lost her? Already, Maddy could see that his face was etched with worry.

As the wagon rumbled closer to town, Maddy became absorbed by the scene unfolding in front of her. They passed a row of large brick houses surrounded by iron fences. Across the street, a white, clapboard church hung back from the road, its sharp thin steeple rising above a set of pines. Nearer to the village, wooden sidewalks ran along both sides of the street. Clare slowed the horse to a walk as they neared the stores. In the mounting heat of the summer morning, Maddy watched merchants roll out awnings and adjust shades on their store windows. Suddenly, as the wagon turned the corner, a loud clang from a blacksmith's anvil startled the horse. It jerked forward.

"Whoa, boy!" Clare steered the wagon to the side of the road in front of a grocery store. He tethered the horse to a post, patted its neck, and then hoisted a crate of soap onto his shoulders.

"Wait here," he said.

Groaning, she slouched on the hard, wooden seat. Behind her, the morning sunshine pressed its hot fingers on her neck. Sweat began to trickle down her back. Across the road, she spotted a large, round fountain that dripped water into a shallow pool. With a jolt, she realized it was the same park from her own time, but it looked quite different. There were dirt paths instead of cement sidewalks crisscrossing its oasis of trees and grass. And in the far corner, the playground with its swings was missing.

Maddy glanced at the grocery store expecting Clare to reappear momentarily. But after a few minutes, she slid off the wagon seat and darted across the dirt road towards the fountain. After splashing water on her face and neck, she flopped on the grass. A boy whizzed past on a bicycle with fat tires that bounced him up and down over the uneven ground. He disappeared into a grove of trees where Maddy was certain the town hall and library had stood the other day. She rolled on her side and peered again at the grocery store. Bright sunshine sliced through the alley next to it. It spotlit the faded words *Sanders Soap* painted above a large yellow soap bar on the side of the building.

Maddy stared at the image and wondered if Clare was having any luck selling his soap. And if he was and he had to hand over every last penny to Uncle Ray, how would he ever be able to buy a train ticket? As she twirled a clump of grass in her fingers, a familiar, pungent scent tickled her nose. It came from a large clump of lavender growing in a nearby flowerbed. All at once, an idea popped into her head. Maybe there was a better way to sell Sanders Soap. A way to "increase sales," as her mother's magazine editor was so fond of saying. She sat up and thought a minute longer before jumping to her feet and retracing her steps across the road to the grocery store.

From its doorway, she scanned the long, narrow interior of Coyle's Grocery Store. Pyramids of cans filled the shelves on each side of the room. A glass case near the door displayed cheeses. In front of it, baskets of apples, carrots, and onions crowded the floor. On its wooden countertop, a metal cash register with two rows of fat keys shared space with jars of licorice and candy sticks. In the middle of the room, behind a black pot-bellied stove, Maddy spotted Clare. A tall man with a white apron wrapped around his thin frame, leaned towards him.

"Sorry son, but all they want is the new soap from the city." The man pointed to a display of boxes and wrapped bars. On the wall hung a bright poster of a woman pinning laundry onto a clothesline. The red letters *Buy Sunlight Soap* danced above her head.

"Our soap cleans clothes just as well as that stuff," Clare said.

"That may be, son. But the ladies are hooked on Sunlight Soap. Claim it smells like sunshine." The grocer threw up his hands. "Tell you what. I'll keep carrying Sanders Soap for a while longer. But I can't promise you anything.

79

Times are changing. Best tell your uncle to make something diff'rent in that factory."

He gave Clare a pat on the shoulder. "Do me a favor, son. One of my wagon wheels needs repairing. I'll pay you a nickel to deliver Mrs. Young's groceries up Pine Street. She wants flour and sugar for her cakes today. Company's coming."

With a grim nod, Clare slid the coin in his pocket and picked up the bags of groceries next to the counter.

Chapter 13

Neither Clare nor Maddy spoke a word as the horse pulled the wagon onto the dusty road and circled the park. They passed a square, yellow brick building with the words *Windsor Hotel* sparkling like gold on its double glass doors. Ornate, iron balconies adorned the second floor with elegant curves and spirals. As a breeze sprang up and ruffled the curtains of a corner window, Maddy glimpsed a young woman's hand reach out and pull the glass shut.

Further along down the narrow, rutted road they passed simple clapboard houses surrounded by picket fences. In the distance, on top of a hill, an imposing brick building loomed out of a row of dark pine trees. Its three stories of tall windows reflected a sky filling with dark clouds. From its height, the austere mansion overlooked the town like the prim headmistress of a boarding school overseeing charges huddled below. Maddy shivered. The sun no longer shone hot on her back. She twisted around and caught sight of thunderclouds rolling up from the lake. A gust of wind whooshed past her and frenziedly shook the leaves of a nearby tree.

"Clare, how far is it to Mrs. Young's place?"

He pointed ahead at a house with a wrap-around veranda. When the wagon finally pulled into its driveway, a bosomy woman with hair tucked in a bun rushed down the steps.

"Thank heavens, you're here," she said, thrusting open the gate with floury hands. "I was worried you wouldn't arrive before the storm."

She reached for a bag of groceries from the wagon. "Ellen and the children are coming on the ten o'clock train. I'm afraid they'll be caught in the rain." She hurried back towards the porch. "Best shelter your horse and wagon by the Windsor till the storm passes."

Clare followed her with the second bag. With a tip of his cap he returned to the wagon. From under the seat, he unhurriedly pulled a ragged canvas tarp and tucked it around the remaining soap crates. On top, he carefully lodged a long-handled axe. Another gust of wind blew up the road. More and darker clouds tumbled above their heads.

"Clare," Maddy cried, "let's go! I don't want to get stuck in this storm." She rubbed her arms up and down, glad now of her long sleeves. Clare tugged his cap tight on his head, slowly turned the wagon around, and guided the horse up the hill away from town.

"Clare! Where are we going? We've got to get out of this storm!"

"Can't spend money parking the horse in the livery stable and staying in a hotel when we can stop up the road for nothing."

Maddy slumped back in her seat. Thunder rolled in the distance. The wind blew cold on her neck. Her heart thumped under the thin cotton of her dress. She feared that getting soaked even on a hot day would set off another round of coughing, maybe even bronchitis. A familiar tightening squeezed her throat. Why hadn't she brought her puffer with her?

"Hold your hat!"

Just in time, Maddy grabbed her straw hat. A burst of wind pushed them onward. The trees on both sides of the road began to sway. Clare slapped the reins on the horse, urging it faster up the hill. The thunder rumbled closer, and as the wind picked up force, it reverberated in longer and closer peals. A streak of lightening split the clouds above them, followed by a loud clap that lifted Maddy off her seat.

"Clare, stop!" She tugged on his arm.

He shook her hand off. "Can't stop here! It ain't safe under the trees with the lightning." He pulled on the reins and turned the wagon down a narrow lane. The wind moaned in the tall pines on either side. Large drops of rain splattered on their heads. The sky darkened to black and then a blast of wind pelted them with a downpour that instantly drenched their clothes. Clare bent over and pressed the horse forward with a slap of the reins. Through the downpour, an opening in the trees appeared. A half minute later they emerged into a clearing. Ahead, a tall, brick house loomed out of the darkness. Maddy recognized its daunting height and large windows. It was the three-story mansion on the hill she had seen earlier.

Clare steered them around the front of the house and

under a carriage porch. He jumped down and tied the horse to a hitching post.

"We can shelter here till the storm passes." He pointed to a small veranda with walls and windows on two sides.

Maddy raced up the steps and huddled by the door. Her teeth chattered. She craved warmth and a blanket to wrap around her soaked body.

"Is anyone home?"

Clare shook his head. Another gust of wind drove the rain sideways and under their small refuge. He pushed against the locked door and rattled its knob.

"Clare, I'm freezing! Try another door!"

"Wait here," he commanded and disappeared into the rain. Maddy wrapped her arms around her chest and watched the tall pines sway in the wind. The day that had started balmy and inviting had turned chilly and threatening. Though Maddy suspected they were not far from home, she felt worlds away in a foreign and frightening place. She listened for Clare's footsteps wishing she was back in her own time, warm and dry on the patio, reading a book, happily bored under the shade of the maples. She shivered uncontrollably and feared that if she stayed here she was going to get really sick. Just like Eva.

Behind her, the door opened suddenly and Maddy tumbled into a dark vestibule. Clare reached to steady her. The touch of his cool fingers felt like ice and fire. She pulled away and shivered even more.

"Here," he said as he thrust a large rough towel at her. Maddy grabbed it and rubbed her dripping hair. Then she wrapped it around her shoulders. The tightness in her chest began to ease.

"How did you get in?"

"Through a window. In the servants' quarters."

Clare motioned Maddy to follow him into the house.

"Should we take off our boots?" she asked when she saw their muddy footprints on the floor.

"Nah, don't worry! Nobody's here."

He stepped forward and pushed open a door into a large octagonal hall. Maddy gasped. High above them, a dim, watery light tumbled through a glass skylight and spilled onto the floor. It illuminated vast scenes of summer and winter painted on the rounded walls. When they entered the hall, Maddy spun slowly on her heels, staring at the murals, her mouth open in a silent "oh!" In one mural a large white rabbit stood on its hind legs. In another, a fawn and its mother nibbled on grass. As she turned around, a white horse reared up in front of her, its rider a soldier brandishing a sword. She yelped and hopped backwards.

Clare's laugh echoed in the hallway. "He's something, ain't he? Scared me the first time I saw him!"

"You've been here before?"

"A coupla times. Deliv'ring wood and things. The old guy who built this place was related to Aunt Ella's mother. A cousin, or something like that. Kendall was his name."

Maddy didn't move. She was fascinated by the murals. High above their heads the rain pounded on the skylight, bathing the hall in a soft glow. She felt as if she had stepped into a life-size snow globe where light shimmered around her. She half-expected to see the rabbit's nose twitch or the fawn lift a delicate leg towards its mother. Then she noticed the carved, wooden doors between the murals. She turned towards Clare. He was watching her, a tiny smile twitching the corner of his mouth.

Without a word, he walked to the closest door and swung it open. It revealed an enormous room with a black, marble fireplace dominating its far side. A magnificent ebony table claimed the middle of the room. Above it hung a glass chandelier with layers of candle holders circling its center globe. In a far corner stood a grand piano. It too was ebony. Maddy gaped at the room in astonishment.

"Is this a ballroom?"

"Could be. They threw big parties up here in my grandparents' time. Pretty grand, ain't it?"

Maddy closed her eyes and imagined women and men twirling to music, like the couple on top of Grammy Bea's music box. How divine it would be to attend just one of the balls held in this room. But before she could imagine another detail, Clare retreated into the hall and towards another door. Reluctantly, Maddy followed him.

The next door revealed the parlor room. It was almost as magical, but smaller, with windows that stretched high above a man's head. These were the panes that had stared down at Maddy while she rode beside Clare in the wagon. Through their wavy glass, Maddy glimpsed white caps on the distant lake. It seemed as if the sky had lightened. Only a misty rain fell on the pine trees nearby. She turned and gazed at the room. Bookcases lined its walls. Two bulky sofas flanked a green, marble fireplace. Enormous plush chairs sat nearby. All the furniture was covered in white sheets.

"To keep the dust off," Clare said as he led the way to another room across the hallway.

This was the dining room. From one side to the other stretched a long, mahogany table with high-backed chairs.

A brass chandelier hung over its center. Dark wood paneled the room from top to bottom. It reminded Maddy of a castle scene in a movie where royalty ate from fine china while butlers hovered at their elbows waiting to pour wine into crystal tumblers. Who were the people who had lived in this mansion? Where had they gone?

"Clare, wait a minute," she began as he pushed open the heavy door to the hallway. "What happened to the owners of this mansion? Where did they go?"

"The colonel died years ago. Last month ole Mrs. Kendall went to live with her daughter in Kingston. Me and Uncle Ray been asked to look after this place till the family makes up their minds about selling it."

"Why would they sell this place? Wouldn't it be wonderful to live here? Think of all the parties you could have! Fancy suppers in the dining room! Dances in the ballroom! And when it's dark outside, that room with the big fireplace would be great for hanging out with friends or for sleepovers."

Maddy twirled around in the soft afternoon glow falling from the skylight above their heads. "Hey Clare, you and Eva should move in here with your mother! After all, you're related to the owners, aren't you?"

Clare grinned at Maddy's exuberance. "Yeah, this place sure is grand," he replied as he glanced at the murals surrounding them. "But I don't believe Mother would be comfortable living here. It's a house for rich people, Maddy. Not folks like us. Not ones with no money."

"Why not? There's tons of room."

"That's just it. This place takes lots of servants to keep it going. Cooks to make meals. Butlers to serve 'em. Maids to dust and clean and wash the clothes. A whole slew of folks to look after the animals and trim the gardens. Aunt Ella told me there was up to two dozen servants working here to keep just Colonel and Mrs. Kendall alive."

"Wow!" Maddy said. "You'd have to be super rich to pay all those people." She paused before adding, "My mom couldn't afford even a cleaning person when we lived in the city. But I wish she'd get somebody to help her with the housework now 'cause she's too tired to do anything most of the time. Dan usually washes the dishes at night so Mom can rest, but he's always on my back . . ." Maddy's words trailed away.

Clare leaned against the door frame. "You don't like Dan much," he stated matter-of-factly.

"Nope."

"Why not? Is he mean to you? Does he beat you?"

"Good Lord, no! Why would he do that?" Maddy stared at Clare, her eyes wide with shock that he should ask such a question.

"Maybe for giving him a hard time about your responsibilities?"

"I help out," she protested. She was embarrassed that Clare had realized she detested chores. He probably always pitched in when asked, but was that because he was threatened?

"Does Uncle Ray hit you, Clare? He seems pretty crabby most of the time."

"Crabby?" Clare looked puzzled. "If you mean gruff, that's just his nature, but he's never raised a hand against me."

"Well, that's good to know." Dan could be pretty gruff

too, but he wasn't mean, at least not like that.

Clare continued to look at her with an air of expectation. Maddy knew she hadn't answered his question about Dan. She bit her lip, unsure of what to tell him.

After a moment of silence, she sighed. Then in a rush, she blurted, "Well, it's like this. Last year, all of a sudden, he showed up in our life and grabbed Mom's attention. All the time. Nobody asked me if I wanted him around. But there he was. And then Mom got pregnant with his baby and now she's always tired and she never has energy for doing stuff with me. . . ."

Maddy's words trailed away before she added in a small voice, "And the other day she said she doesn't want to help me find my real dad."

"Your real dad? You mean the one that ran off when you were a just a kid?"

"Yeah, him. I want to find him. I bet he's a lot nicer than Dan."

Clare shook his head. "If he was such a good father, he wouldn't have left you."

"How do you know that?" The words slipped out of Maddy's mouth before she remembered that Clare's father had also disappeared.

Clare frowned and, without a word, stepped into the octagonal hallway. He stopped by the mural of the soldier with the sword. Daylight filtered down through the glass far above his head, exposing the anger in his eyes. Maddy watched him warily from the doorway.

"Good fathers provide for their children," Clare stated with utter conviction. "My father took off out West when Eva and I were real small. Left Mother with no means to raise two children. Said he would send money, but he never did. Now Eva's real sick and he still don't come back."

The fierceness in Clare's words surprised Maddy. He always seemed so even-tempered. She wasn't sure how to answer him.

"Sometimes my dad sent me stuff . . . like postcards . . . when I was four or five." Her voice trailed away.

Clare ignored her feeble defense of her father. "Dan seems like a decent man. He puts a roof over your head, like Uncle Ray does for me. Don't he put food in your belly too? And make sure you have clothes and money for schoolin'? Can't ask for much more."

Maddy scuffed the door-jamb with her shoe. In light of Clare's opinions, her antipathy towards Dan seemed pretty flimsy. "Well," she replied, "I get the feeling he's just putting up with me most of the time."

"Do you sass him?"

"Yeah, sometimes. I can't help it. He's so bossy!"

Clare smiled. "Well, there ya go, Maddy. Uncle Ray don't tolerate sass and I bet your Dan don't like it either."

"No, he sure doesn't." Maddy said with a wry grin. "But I'd like it if he was nicer to me, if you know what I mean."

"Like I told you, Dan's same as Uncle Ray, not a friendly feller, but a decent one. Ya gotta toughen up, Maddy. Appreciate what you have in life. It ain't so bad."

Maddy nodded uncertainly. Deep down, she knew Clare was right. Dan worked hard at his job and he fixed up their house on weekends. It was obvious, if she admitted it, that he loved her mother and that her mother loved him. If only he wasn't so pushy and acted kinder to her. Well, Maddy sighed inwardly, she'd think about what Clare had said, but she wasn't convinced Dan felt more than toleration for her. And she wasn't about to give up on finding her father.

"Storm's moving away," Clare announced as he glanced at the skylight. "Best be getting on." He strode towards the porch door.

Maddy hesitated and then called after him, "Clare, wait a minute. I forgot to tell you about my great idea for selling Sanders Soap!"

Chapter 14

Before Clare could protest, Maddy sat down on the marble bench beneath the summer mural. She patted the seat and he reluctantly perched on its edge. In a rush of words, she described her mother's handmade soap project.

"Mom said her recipe uses soap that's already made. You just melt it and add lavender flowers, like the ones in her garden. That's all I remember. But I could find the recipe and bring the ingredients to your factory. We could make this new soap together! What do you think?"

Clare frowned. "Why'd we do that? We got lots of soap already. And it's not selling."

"To make money, Clare! So you can buy a train ticket and bring the antibiotics to Eva!"

"How can I sell that new soap if I can't sell what we already got?"

Maddy jumped up and paced impatiently around the octagonal hall.

"Clare, we'd make much better soap. The kind people like 'cause it smells fantastic." She stopped in front of the rabbit and deer painted on the wall.

"Listen, you could make special molds, octagon ones." Maddy's head spun with ideas. "We could paint rabbits and deer on the wrapping paper. And give it a special name. Maybe after this mansion. Does it have a name?"

"Kendallwood."

"There you have it! Kendallwood Soap! Everyone will love it. It'll remind them of this house where they danced in that enormous ballroom and ate scrumptious meals in the dining room! You'll sell lots and make tons of money!"

Clare's eyes widened with astonishment.

"C'mon, Clare! It's a great idea!" Excited by her rising enthusiasm, she dropped onto the bench next to him. "Listen, in my mom's magazine, there's tons of ads for fancy soaps. People buy them all the time! We even have some cute, little perfumed ones in our bathroom."

"Well," he swallowed. "You sure have plenty of ideas, Maddy. But you're right, people do buy fancy things. And this house is about as fancy as it gets. Guess we could try something diff'rent."

A late afternoon sun broke through the clouds and lit the hallway as Maddy and Clare planned their new soap project. She promised to copy the recipe and harvest lavender flowers from the garden. He agreed to scrounge up a pot for melting soap and to make octagonal molds.

Then Maddy groaned. "Oh no! What if Shadow doesn't show up and the door in the attic won't open?"

"That cat can't open doors by herself," Clare snorted. "She's always scratching for someone to let her in or out."

But when Maddy frowned, he reassured her that he'd find the cat and chase her into the attic so Maddy could return to her own time.

"I ain't seen that attic door yet, but you seem to disappear most of the time, so I 'spect it's somewhere up there." The corners of Clare's mouth twitched. "Stop your fretting and let's get going 'fore my folks 'spect something's wrong."

Maddy turned towards him, her eyebrows raised. Was he teasing her? Clare stared back. She noticed his thick eyelashes again, and a laugh in his eyes. She suspected he didn't believe a word of her story, but she didn't care. He was cute when he smiled. With that thought she felt her face grow warm. She quickly glanced away and then stood up and headed for the outside door, Clare following behind her.

The ride home was quiet, almost too quiet, as Clare retreated into his usual silence. He had chosen a road north of the village that wound past farms and woods. At first, while they bumped along, Maddy worried about finding the cat, and the soap recipe, and all the right ingredients. Then she worried about Eva. Would their plan work? Would Eva get better? But after a while, Maddy's racing thoughts slowed down and she caught sight of a crow drinking from a puddle in the ditch. In the corner of a field, she glimpsed a deer munching grass. A rabbit scurried across the road. With the western sun warm on her back, peace settled into her body, and she no longer minded Clare's silence. The slow clip clop of the horse's hooves lulled her into a drowsy sleep.

Suddenly the wagon stopped with a jolt that nearly knocked Maddy off the seat. Her eyes flew open as she grabbed the side of the wagon. An uprooted poplar tree with a forest of branches blocked their way. Clare jumped down and lifted the axe out of the wagon. With practiced swings, he hacked at the nearest branch. Maddy scrambled off the wagon, grabbed the heavy limb, and dragged it to the side of the road, surprised by her own strength. They worked together for half an hour, clearing enough branches to allow passage for the wagon. With each step, Maddy's breath flowed evenly in and out of her lungs.

"Thanks," Clare grinned. "You're stronger than you look."

Maddy smiled back. "Guess it's all the fresh air." She climbed onto the wagon bench and wiped the sweat off her face. She glanced sideways at Clare and saw a smile still lighting his face. A warm glow filled her heart. It would be great working together.

When they reached home, Maddy hopped out of the wagon north of the barn and waited in the shadow of a tall cedar tree for Clare's all-clear whistle. She slipped past the barn, and tiptoed through the silent, darkened kitchen and up the steps into the attic. There, curled on the bed, slept the black cat, the white tip of her tail tucked between her paws.

"Where have you been, Shadow?" Maddy hissed. The cat peered at her through half-opened eyes. She lifted her head and, for a second, stared past Maddy before resuming her nap. Maddy spun around and saw the outline of a small door in the wall.

"Phew!" she breathed. Then, on the floor, she spotted her running shoes plopped on top of each other, like two dead mice. That was weird. She thought she'd left them in the barn. Did Shadow drag them upstairs? In too much of a hurry to think about it, Maddy unbuttoned the sleeves of the crumpled dress and pulled it over her head. As she hung it on the hook, she checked its pocket for the sock with the pills. Still there! She tucked them under the pillow next to Shadow.

"Take good care of them," she whispered to the cat. "They're going to make Eva better."

Dressed in her jeans and T-shirt, she slipped on her shoes and pushed open the door into her own time. How was she going to explain her long absence? She had been gone almost two whole days. Her mother would be frantic with worry. Dan the Man would be furious. Maddy listened for the crackle of a police radio in the driveway. The only sound she heard was the faint beep-beep-beep of the microwave in the kitchen below. The light in the woodshed grew brighter. Was it evening or early morning?

In the kitchen, Dan sipped a cup of steaming coffee. He didn't look upset. In fact, he greeted Maddy with a smile. "You're up early. Where've you been?"

"Looking for a cat," she mumbled, avoiding his eyes. She had no idea what day it was in her own time, but she was ravenously hungry. She filled a bowl with cereal and milk and ate her breakfast in silence, not once looking up. Behind her, she felt Dan's eyes on her back. But when he finished his coffee, he left the kitchen without another word. Relieved, Maddy slipped into the living room and shuffled through the magazines and books piled on the coffee table until she found *Making Your Own Soap*. She tiptoed up to her bedroom and shoved the book into her backpack. From her dresser she pocketed coins for the photocopy machine at the library and a candy bar from the store. Back in the kitchen, she bent to tie her shoelaces before heading out the door.

"Now where are you off to?"

Maddy jumped. Where had Dan come from?

"For a bike ride," she said.

"Carla isn't feeling well today. I think you should stay home and help her."

"What's wrong with her?"

"She's exhausted. Didn't sleep well last night."

Maddy bit back the words *well, maybe you snored too much* and instead asked, "Well, what do you want me to do?"

"Empty the dishwasher. Do a load of laundry. Water the garden. Whatever Carla needs."

Maddy groaned. She knew she had to tackle a few chores. Wasn't that what Clare had hinted at in the mansion? But now, when her head was full of plans and she was itching to bike to the library?

She took a deep breath. "Okay, Dan. But first I got something real important to do. I'll just be gone a little while and then I'll help Mom."

Without waiting for his reply, Maddy hoisted her backpack onto her shoulder, pushed open the door, and headed to her bike in the garage.

Chapter 15

The cool morning air ruffled Maddy's hair as she pedaled past the old maple trees and bungalows lining her street. Here and there, she spotted the brick houses she had seen the day before when she bumped down the road in the wagon. But all their barns were gone, replaced by paved driveways and cramped backyards. Instead of swallows swooping over hay fields, mourning doves perched overhead on telephone wires, cooing their sad songs to anyone who passed below.

When she turned onto the road leading into town, Maddy searched for the General Store where Clare had unloaded a crate of soap the day before. Which one of these old buildings was it? The run-down one with the big picture window? The other one with the sagging front porch? Maddy couldn't tell. Across the street, the furniture store had disappeared. In its place an empty garage slumped on crumbling cinder blocks. Only the brick Baptist church looked familiar, but it too stood vacant and abandoned. She wondered how Clare would feel about everything looking so run-down.

Closer to town, Maddy recognized the grand, old houses from yesterday. The row of stores on the north side of the town also looked familiar too, even though modern signs were mounted above their windows and metal siding covered the brickwork. In front of them, instead of horses hitched to a wooden rail, cars lined the asphalt street.

Maddy steered her bike onto a concrete sidewalk. All the stores were closed. She stopped and peered into the pharmacy's window. A clock on the wall read 8:40. Had she missed a whole day and a night's sleep? With that thought, a wave of exhaustion swept over her.

Dragging her feet, she walked her bike to the park and collapsed onto the bench next to the tiered fountain. She wondered what happened to the big one with the round pool. A fog of confusion began to swirl around her. Was it just yesterday that horses and buggies had kicked up dust as they rounded the corners of the park? Now tires screeched to a stop and then picked up speed before leaving town. Was it just yesterday that merchants had rolled up awnings over their store windows? Now some guy was wheeling a rack of shovels in front of a hardware store. And where was Coyle's Grocery Store, which had bustled with customers? Now the shabby building's empty windows reflected only the sky. Maddy felt dizzy. She closed her eyes and fell into a light sleep.

"Hey Janine, look! That girl's sleeping on the bench!"

Maddy struggled up. A girl her age stood in front of her, holding the hand of a small boy.

"You okay?"

Maddy rubbed her eyes. "Yeah. Didn't get much sleep last night."

"Me neither. We just moved here yesterday. I had to share a bed with my brother, and he kicks a lot."

"You snore!"

The girl tousled her brother's hair. "No I don't!"

She waved her hand towards the north side of the park. "We're going to Mr. Convenience for Freezies. Want to come?"

Maddy peered across the park. The scene was surreal. Yesterday, the Windsor Hotel had majestically spread itself over the whole block. Today, a convenience store squatted there surrounded by a narrow parking lot. She felt like an untethered balloon floating between past and present. When a breeze parted the tree leaves, a hot sunbeam grazed the back of her neck. She jerked round and saw a large S shimmering on the pharmacy's brick wall. Below it, an outline of a bar of soap flickered like a fluorescent sign. Maddy gasped. Then stammered, "I've gotta get to the library."

"Well, come over later. My name's Janine. We live on the street by the school. You'll see my dad's boat in the driveway."

Boat? New in town? Maddy wondered if this was the girl Dan had mentioned at supper. The one whose father worked with him building houses on the other side of town. The one whose family invited them for supper on their sailboat. Dan would be pleased if Maddy accepted her invitation, but now was not the time. She had a job to do. Clare was waiting.

Maddy mumbled that she couldn't stay and, with a

quick "bye," wheeled her bike to the town hall where the librarian was climbing the steps. In response to her cheery "good morning," Maddy asked if she could use the photocopy machine right away. Five minutes later, she stuffed the copied pages into her backpack and pushed open the heavy, oak door, almost bumping into an elderly woman sliding books into the library return box.

"Sorry," she mumbled.

"You're out early, Maddy Rose. Do be careful today. Nothing foolish, okay?"

Maddy gaped at her. Was that her neighbor? How did she know her name? Or for that matter, her plans? Without a reply, she shifted her pack onto her back and wheeled her bike to the street. Pedling away from town, she wobbled along the road. Maybe she was too tired to do this soap thing with Clare. Maybe she'd mess it all up. Or maybe Shadow wouldn't be around and the door to the attic would be closed. But when Maddy stashed her bike in the woodshed, two yellow eyes peered down at her from the loft. She took a deep breath. She had to hurry.

In the house, Carla sipped tea at the kitchen table. Dark circles ringed her eyes.

"You went out early," she said, yawning.

Maddy filled a glass of water and gulped it down. "I went for a bike ride," she replied with a small burp.

"Excuse me!"

Maddy wiped her mouth. "'Scuse me."

Carla pushed her uncombed hair away from her face. "I'm glad you came home early, Maddy. Dan says it's going to be a scorcher today, and I could use an extra pair of hands around here."

Maddy slipped the backpack off her shoulder and balanced it between her legs. Her mother did look exhausted, slouched in her chair, her head resting on one hand. What should she do? Stay home and help her mom? Maddy instinctively knew that was the right thing to do, but what would Clare think if she didn't show up in the mill? Would he wonder if she had deserted him? And then what? Since he couldn't make lavender soap without her, he'd have no choice but to abandon their project. Then Eva would never get the pills that could cure her. Maddy closed her eyes for a moment and then took a deep breath.

"Mom," she said. "I met a new girl this morning. She just moved here. I think her dad works with Dan. And she's invited me to her house. Can I go there soon? Before it's too hot? For just an hour or two?"

"Well, okay," Carla replied wearily. "I'm glad you found a new friend, but please try to be back in time for lunch." She pushed herself out of her chair and rubbed her belly with both hands. "This baby kept me awake all night," she said. "I'm going to rest on the patio before the sun heats it up."

Maddy watched her mother shuffle with an unsteady gait across the kitchen floor. "Need anything, Mom?" she called after her. "More tea?"

Carla nodded.

Maddy quickly picked up her mother's empty cup. She refilled it and added a few drops of milk just the way her mother liked it. Then she popped bread in the toaster, cut up an apple, and hastily arranged the breakfast on a tray which she carried to the patio where Carla had curled up on a lounge chair.

"Need anything else?"

"The throw from the living room couch would be nice."

Maddy fetched it while returning the soap book to the coffee table. After she tucked the crocheted blanket over her mother's legs, she promised to be back in time to make everyone lunch. Then she slipped into the bathroom and scooped the lavender oil off the shelf.

A voice in Maddy's head reminded her to check the recipe so she wouldn't forget anything. Sure enough, she needed the box of oatmeal from the kitchen cupboard. Maddy stuffed it, plus a grater and a measuring cup, into her backpack. From the bottom drawer of the hutch, she pulled out tissue paper and ribbon, which she put in a separate bag so as not to crush them.

In the garden she located the lavender plants and snipped a bag full of blossoms. Through the patio's screen door she shouted, "Bye, Mom!"

She hoped she'd be back in time for lunch as she had promised. How long could it take to make a batch of soap? Maddy hadn't a clue, and she knew time between the two worlds seldom matched, but she was too excited to give it much thought as she headed towards the loft and the door to the attic.

Chapter 16

In no time at all, Maddy found herself in the old kitchen, listening for voices. Where was Clare? She tiptoed to the living room in the octagon. Overhead, footsteps padded softly across a bedroom floor. Certain they were not Clare's, Maddy hurried out the back door to the barn. But it was empty. Even the horse was gone.

Across the road, she noticed a large rock propping open the mill door. She ran to it and peered cautiously into its enormous, jumbled interior. An unwelcome, foul smell greeted her nose. When her eyes adjusted to the mill's dim light, she spotted Clare stirring a large iron pot on the wood stove. He turned towards her. A frown passed over his face like a small, dark cloud.

"Back so soon?"

"That was the plan." Maddy dropped her backpack on the wooden floor with a deliberate thud. "Why are you doing that again?" she asked with annoyance. "We're supposed to make our lavender soap today. Not that awful stuff." The excited anticipation of working with Clare threatened to fizzle out of her like air from a slow tire leak. She sank into a barrel next to a table away from the stove. Her breakfast churned in her stomach.

"Gotta render this pig fat 'fore it goes bad."

"Smells like it already did. It's making me sick."

Clare shrugged. "Uncle Ray got a special order for a barrel of soft soap, so he told me to boil up this lard 'fore he left with Aunt Helen. They're meeting with the lawyer in town about this ole mill."

"Well, I hope they're gone a long time 'cause we've got work to do." Maddy hoisted her backpack onto the wooden table, unzipped it, and pulled out the recipe. "Here are the instructions for lavender soap." She thumped the backpack with determination. "All the ingredients are here, except the soap. And the wrapping paper I left on the bed in the attic."

Clare pointed to the drying racks. "Soap's over there. Help yourself. I gotta keep stirring so this fat don't burn." He glanced at her running shoes. "You don't have boots on, so watch your step!"

"Nope. Forgot about them." She marched across the room, chose two large blocks of soap, and dropped them on the table. While Clare stirred the pot, she smoothed out the recipe with slow swipes of her hand, hoping to calm her irritation.

"Okay, Clare, first we've got to measure the ingredients. Here's the lavender oil. We need two ounces." Maddy squinted at the label on the bottle. "There's four ounces in here, so I guess we'll use half."

Clare kept stirring. Maddy sighed and pulled out the

bag of lavender. "I'd better pick off these stems 'cause we don't want anything scratchy in the soap."

"Do what you gotta do. I can't stop. But soon I could use your help straining this lard."

"I'm not touching that stuff!" Maddy said dropping lavender blossoms, one by one, into a pile. Working with Clare didn't seem as wonderful as she had anticipated.

"Got any bowls? We need a big one for the soap and a little one for the oatmeal. And how 'bout a double boiler? And some clean water?"

"Don't sound like a soapmaking recipe to me."

"We're not making the soap, Clare." Maddy gritted her teeth. "We're just melting it and adding new ingredients to create better soap. Soap that sells!"

Clare snorted, but pointed to a small cupboard near the stove. In it she found bowls and two pots, one small enough to fit on top of the other. On the floor next to the stove sat a pail of water. It seemed clean. Maddy returned to the instructions.

"Hey, Clare," she called with a bright smile, "we have to grate these humongous blocks of soap! How do I do that?"

"Guess I could cut 'em up, if you stir this lard."

Maddy's eyes narrowed, but she edged close to the wood stove and glanced into the pot. Big, lazy bubbles rose to the surface of its thick, yellow mass. Pinching her nose, she took the wooden stick from Clare and poked at the mixture while he chopped the soap blocks into smaller chunks. Suddenly a large bubble popped and splattered hot grease on Maddy's arm. With a shriek, she jumped back and bumped into Clare. His knife clattered to the floor.

"Careful! Don't knock that kettle over!"

"It burned me!"

Maddy rubbed her arm. Then she saw Clare holding his left hand. A drop of blood seeped through his fingers. Her eyes widened.

"Just skin off my knuckle. Hand me that cloth." Clare tore off a strip with his teeth and wrapped his thumb. Without looking at her, he retrieved the stir stick from the floor.

In awkward silence, they traded places and Maddy began to grate the smaller chunks of soap into the bowl. Working together was more challenging than she imagined. For some reason, Clare had again retreated into himself. He seemed uninterested in their project. Discouragement settled on her like a heavy cloak. Maybe this wasn't such a great idea. She rubbed the back of her neck. Maybe she should just give up and go home. With a dejected sigh she jerked the soap on the grater and scraped her knuckle.

"Ow!" She popped it into her mouth and then spit it out. "Yuck! Tastes like soap!"

Clare's mouth twitched while his eyes lit up with laughter. Maddy wiped her mouth and waved a finger at him.

"We're even now," she said with a tight grin.

The tension between them began to evaporate like the steam from the kettle and they returned to their work. After weighing the grated soap on a scale, Maddy arranged the bowls on the table.

"Everything's ready for melting the soap."

"Gotta finish this job first."

"Okay."

With a few instructions from Clare, they carefully strained the melted lard through a loosely woven cloth into a clean bucket and carried it to a cool corner in the back of the mill.

"Here, taste this." Clare picked a browned crumble from the cloth and handed it to her. "It's cracklin'. Roasted pig skin."

Maddy wrinkled her nose, but bit off a piece. "Hey! Not bad! Like potato chips!"

Clare dropped another one onto her palm. While they munched the crackling, he confessed he hadn't built new, octagonal molds. Maddy admitted she hadn't made the special wrapping paper, though she had left her mother's tissue paper and ribbon on the bed in the attic.

Then, side by side, they studied the steps for making lavender soap. First they poured water in the bottom of the double boiler and measured more into its top pan. After it had heated on the stove, Maddy carefully dropped in the grated soap and began to stir with a wooden spoon. Seated at the table, Clare opened his pocketknife and scraped the old soap out of Uncle Ray's square molds.

As Maddy stood by the stove, sweat beaded on her forehead. Soon her arm tired. She tried to stir with her left hand. When she changed hands again, her arm brushed the top of the hot stove. With a yelp, she jerked away, jostling the pan.

"Careful," Clare cautioned. "Like I told you, it's hard work."

Maddy swallowed a retort and stepped back from the hot metal. Trying hard to pay attention, she kept a close eye on the soap so it melted smoothly without bubbling. She stirred and stirred until her arms ached. She was glad she didn't have to make soap every day. After all their hard work, they'd better sell every last bar.

Twenty minutes later, the melted soap had absorbed all the water and began to string. First it looked like cottage cheese. Then like lumpy marshmallow cream.

"I think it's ready now!" she said.

Clare cleared a space on the table for the pan. Then they poured in the lavender oil and the oatmeal. Now the soap was so hard to stir that Clare offered to mix it up.

"It sure smells nice," he said as they spooned it into molds and tapped out the air bubbles. "When it hardens, we can cut 'em into bars."

"Then we'll wrap and sell it! With the fancy paper I left in the attic. By next week we'll be counting our money!"

"'Fraid not, Maddy. Hard'ning takes two weeks."

"That's not what the recipe says! It should be ready by tomorrow."

Maddy pointed to the sheet of instructions. Clare read them and shook his head.

"That don't sound right. Soap always takes two weeks to harden. You sure about those directions?"

Maddy shrugged. "I never made soap before," she said defensively. "But that's what's printed here." She tapped the paper. "Two weeks is way too long to wait! We gotta get those pills to Eva as soon as possible."

"Can't rush soap, Maddy."

Without a reply, she watched Clare carefully carry the molds to the drying rack in the far corner. It seemed that she couldn't rush him either. If he was right, Eva would be gone for the Cure way before he even bought a ticket and boarded the train. A lot of good sitting on a porch in the mountains would do her. Maybe she should buy the train ticket and take the pills to Belleville. By herself. Wearing Eva's dress and boots.

"Cat got your tongue?"

Maddy winced. She looked down at the floor, feeling guilty for even considering another plan.

"Listen, Clare," she said as she gathered the remaining ingredients together. "I'll come back tomorrow to see if our soap has hardened. If it has, we'll wrap it and take it to that little store down the road. If it still needs more time . . ." Maddy hesitated, avoiding his gaze. "Well, let's see what happens."

She reached for the recipe, and as she folded it, she noticed the small note at the bottom of the paper.

"Hey, look!" she said with forced cheerfulness. "Lavender oil's good for cuts and burns." She dabbed a few drops on her burnt arm and skinned knuckle before thrusting the bottle at him.

"Here, try some!"

He held up his bandaged finger and shook his head.

"You smell good, Maddy. Like our soap."

Maddy's face colored. All of a sudden, she felt shy.

"I gotta go, Clare. I'm super tired." She hoisted her backpack onto her shoulder. "Bye!"

As she turned away, her foot skidded on the slippery floor. Clare grabbed her arm.

"Wear your boots next time." He grinned as he steadied her.

"Will do," she mumbled and fled out the door.

Chapter 17

Behind the house, Maddy spotted a wooden box pushed under the creamery window. She climbed onto it and tugged up the sash, rattling its glass. Then she lowered her backpack to the floor.

"Young ladies enter through the door."

Maddy's head jerked up and banged against the window frame. There was Aunt Ella standing by the sink. Rubbing her head, Maddy climbed awkwardly over the windowsill. She looked sheepishly at the old woman.

"Clare . . ."

"He's just like you sneaking in through that window. Eva too." Aunt Ella gestured at the small green door. "Escaping upstairs to hide from chores, they did when they was young," she chuckled. "Muddy footprints gave them away, ev'ry time."

She waved a letter in the air.

"But she won't be coming here any time soon. Going to the States now, to see that fancy doctor."

"Eva?"

Aunt Ella peered at Maddy over her glasses. "Aye, Eva. Martha's taking her to the sanatorium in the mountains." She shook her head. "If she's fit to travel." Aunt Ella folded the letter and tucked it into her pocket.

Maddy's shoulders slumped. She was right. They couldn't wait for the soap to harden for more than a day. They might not even have time for Clare to sell it. She would have to use her own money for Clare's ticket. Or she would have to go by herself.

"Ella! We're home!" Footsteps crossed the kitchen floor.

As Aunt Ella shuffled away to greet Aunt Helen, Maddy fled through the green door into the attic. Shadow lay on the bed. When she saw Maddy, she lifted her head and blinked at the wall. The small door to the woodshed was ajar. Without hesitation, Maddy ducked through it and into her own time.

In the woodshed's loft, a wave of exhaustion rushed over her and pushed her into the captain's chair. She yawned and tried to collect her thoughts. She needed to gather supplies for her train trip—snacks, a bottle of water, maybe a sweatshirt. Certainly money. But what kind? She couldn't buy a ticket with money that had Queen Elizabeth's face on it. Wait a minute! Poppa George had given her an old two-dollar bill for her birthday. It had *Dominion of Canada* stamped across the top in big old-fashioned letters. It was in her Private Box under her bed.

Maddy yawned again. The warm air of the loft began to wrap around her like a blanket. She closed her eyes and, without meaning to, fell asleep.

Hours later, sweat trickled down her forehead and woke her. Where was she? Her hand brushed the backpack scrunched on her lap. She stared at it groggily. Bit by bit, her memory returned in single words. *Eva. Pills. Train.* She jumped up and scrambled down the ladder. When she pushed open the woodshed door, she spotted a familiar car parked next to Dan's truck. In the kitchen, she heard her grandfather's voice on the patio. A surge of excitement shot through Maddy. Maybe Poppa George knew how people used to travel by train, like, a hundred years ago. With a yank, she slid open the screen door so hard it jumped its track

"Poppa George!"

"Whoa! Maddy!" Her grandfather rose from his chair and hugged her. "Where've you been? Carla said you disappeared this morning."

"Uhh, what time is it?"

"Four-thirty, young lady." Dan's voice was tight with disapproval as he wrangled the screen door back onto its track. "You promised your mother you'd be back for lunch."

Maddy gulped and turned towards Carla who was lying on the lounge chair, her crocheted blanket still tucked around her legs. Dark smudges circled under her eyes.

Maddy flashed her a small guilty grin. "I'm real sorry I didn't make it home for lunch, Mom. You okay?"

"I'm feeling better, hon." Carla smiled wanly back at her. "Don't worry. I had a nap this afternoon. I'm fine." She sipped her iced tea. "Dan brought home a cooked chicken and some potato salad for supper. Maybe you could pick lettuce and tomatoes for a green salad?"

Maddy nodded. "You staying for supper?" she asked Poppa George.

"Yup! But after dishes, I'm off to Kingston to visit an old school buddy," he said as he swatted a mosquito on his arm. "I think it's time to move indoors."

While Dan helped Carla into the kitchen, Maddy ran to the garden with her mother's vegetable basket to search for a handful of early tomatoes and some lettuce leaves that hadn't wilted in the hot sun. After they were washed, she set out plates, glasses, and forks for everyone. As she ate, she couldn't stop her legs from jiggling up and down under the table. She could hardly wait to talk to Poppa George in private. But supper seemed to drag on until Dan began to describe his project making gingerbread trim for new houses west of town.

"They're being built on a large piece of land where a famous, old mansion stood long ago," he told Poppa George. "It was struck by lightning during a storm. No one was home, but by the time the firefighters arrived, the house couldn't be saved." Dan leaned back in his chair. "You can still find bricks from the ruins buried in the dirt."

Maddy stopped chewing. An old mansion on a hill? The one with the marvelous paintings and the huge ballroom? It burned down? Maddy swallowed. That sounded disastrous! Maybe they wouldn't be able to sell their Kendallwood Soap even if it had already hardened.

"When did that happen?" she asked Dan in a rush.

"When did what happen?"

"That mansion. When did it burn down?"

Dan scratched his chin. "Not sure. Quite a while ago. Why do you ask?"

When Maddy mumbled "Just curious," Dan suggested that if she was really interested in what had happened, he'd ask one of the older men on his crew if they knew anything about the fire.

"It's no big deal," Maddy replied, not wanting Dan to probe further. He raised a quizzical eyebrow at her, but she glanced away hoping he'd drop the subject. It didn't matter exactly when the mansion had been destroyed. She was sure she had to get on the train to Belleville and find Eva real soon. Like, now.

"Poppa, do you know where the Colebrook train station is . . . or was?"

"Well, let me think. The tracks still run below the county road, so the station would have been south of the stores in town."

"Don't go wandering around looking for it now," Dan said abruptly, reaching for the potato salad. "When CN Rail bought up the train tracks, they tore down the station."

Maddy frowned. Was Dan afraid she was going to bolt out of the house right after supper? She almost retorted, *Don't worry so much*, but instead bit her lip and stared at her plate until the conversation veered away from the topic. After supper, Poppa George suggested they clean up the dishes together. Maddy instantly agreed.

"Nice that you're helping Poppa George," Dan remarked as he packed leftovers into the refrigerator.

Maddy scowled at him behind his back, unsure how to take his comment. Was he truly appreciative of her helping or was he being ever-so-slightly sarcastic? She shrugged and carried the plates and glasses to the counter. As Poppa George stacked them in the dishwasher, she rocked on her heels, wondering how to ask her grandfather the price of a train ticket in the early 1900s.

"Thinking of taking a train somewhere, Maddy?"

Her head jerked up. Had Poppa George read her mind? She cleared her throat.

"Poppa, how much did a train ticket cost a hundred years ago?"

"Well," he replied as he rinsed the greasy chicken platter. "I guess that depends where you were going."

"Oh, not very far," Maddy said hesitantly. "Say, like to Belleville?"

"Probably, not very much. Maybe a dollar or two. Money stretched a long way back then." He turned and looked at her, a twinkle in his eye. "Planning this trip any time soon?"

Maddy's face reddened. She reached for the wooden salad bowl and rubbed it dry with a towel. How could she explain to him about her travels back in time? He'd think she was crazy. He'd tell her mother . . . and Dan. Then they'd think she was crazy and book an appointment with the doctor. By the time she'd got home, it would be too late to help Eva. She had better change the conversation. But before she could help it, she blurted out another question, one that was uppermost in her mind.

"Poppa, in the olden days, did people die from consumption?"

Her grandfather lowered the platter into the rack, reached for another dish towel, and wiped his hands dry before he answered her. "Interesting that you ask, Maddy. As a matter of fact, my Great Uncle George, the one I was named after, came down with consumption when he was a young man."

"You knew someone that had consumption?"

"Oh, I didn't know him. He died before I was born, but not from consumption. Crushed by a falling tree, but that's another story." Poppa George folded an arm across his chest and tapped a finger on his lower lip.

"One summer, when I was a boy, our family vacationed in New York State. I overheard my parents talking about a sanatorium in town built for people who had contracted tuberculosis. That's the disease's real name, Maddy. Tuberculosis. Apparently Great Uncle George stayed at that place, not far from the cottage we rented years later."

"Did your uncle sit on a freezing cold porch dressed in sweaters?"

Poppa George chuckled. "Come to think of it, that's probably exactly what he did. The cure in those days was to eat good food, rest outdoors in the fresh air, and get some exercise. Basically, build up your immune system and pray you could fight off the disease. Must have worked for Great Uncle George, 'cause eventually he did get better."

Maddy wondered if this place in the mountains was Eva's destination.

"Did everybody get better at that sanatorium?"

"Most did. Some didn't," her grandfather said.

Those were Clare's exact words!

"Nothing works all the time, Maddy. Until antibiotics came along, many people died from tuberculosis. Once someone became infected with the bacteria that causes it, it usually lodged in their lungs and created cavities, holes that collected mucous. The poor souls coughed and coughed so hard to get rid of it that they'd spit up blood. Eventually they'd waste away and die."

Maddy shuddered, remembering Eva's coughing fit and the blood on her handkerchief. Was Eva wasting away? Would she die soon? Maddy's chest tightened. There was no time to lose. She had to go back as soon as possible. She wouldn't be gone long. Maybe just overnight. No one would miss her.

Poppa George draped the dish towel over the oven door's handle.

"Well, girl, give me a hug. It's time I got back on the highway."

While her grandfather said goodbye to her mother and Dan, who were watching television in the living room, Maddy emptied the soap supplies from her backpack and returned the lavender oil to the bathroom. Thankful for the roundness of her house, she snuck through Dan's office and climbed the stairs, two at a time, to her bedroom. She quickly stuffed a hoodie and a pair of socks in her backpack. And her puffer . . . just in case.

Then she rummaged under the bed for her Private Box. Inside was the *Dominion of Canada* two-dollar bill enclosed in a hard plastic case. She pried the case open and folded the bill, putting it into her jean pocket. Finally, she was ready to leave. Once she made it to the attic, she would change into Eva's dress, transfer the pills to her backpack, and find Clare. Then off they'd go to the train station. If he wasn't around, she'd figure out a way to go herself.

Outside, she heard Poppa George's car start up and back down the driveway. As quiet as the cat she hoped was waiting for her in the loft, she tiptoed downstairs and out the front door. In less than a minute, she scrambled up the ladder in the woodshed. But the back wall of the loft was dark. Again, the door to the past had disappeared.

Chapter 18

Maddy sank to her knees by the wall. She banged on it and shouted, "Shadow, Shadow, let me in!" She pressed her ear against the boards and listened for sounds from the other side. Silence. Again, she shouted, "Shadow, let me in! Please!"

Again, silence.

Then a faint voice. "Maddy! Maddy! Where are you?"

It was her mother, calling from the kitchen. The kitchen in her own time. She must have heard Maddy's cries through the creamery ceiling. Maddy shrank away from the wall and perched on the edge of the captain's chair. What should she do? She was desperate to return to Clare and Eva's time.

"Maddy, are you stuck somewhere?" The voice was right

below her.

Maddy didn't want her mother or Dan to find her in the woodshed. She dropped her backpack on the chair and slipped down the ladder. Then as fast as possible, she raced to the front of the octagon and let herself in the door.

"Mom?" she called from the living room. "Where are you?"

Dan and her mother appeared in the small hallway between the kitchen and the octagon. Trying to look puzzled, Maddy tilted her head and lifted her eyebrows.

"Something wrong?"

"We heard yelling."

"Not me. I was in my room."

"Well," said her mother. "It sounded like you, but outside."

Maddy shrugged. "Probably someone walking up the road." She turned towards the stairs. "I'm real tired, Mom. I think I'll go to bed early." Dan and Carla exchanged a puzzled glance.

Lying on her bed she wondered how she could sneak into the woodshed again. After a few minutes, she heard her mother and Dan climb the stairs. Their bedroom door closed with a soft click. A moment later, a loud crash rang from their room, followed by a moment of silence, and then laughter. Maddy sat up. Her mother and Dan were giggling. Had their bed collapsed when they climbed into it? Probably. Dan still hadn't attached the bed frame to the headboard. With a groan, Maddy rolled over and pulled the pillow over her head.

*****

The next thing Maddy heard was the persistent whistle

of the cardinal waking her early the next morning. In the driveway, Dan's truck door closed with a click. Then a motor rumbled to life and the truck backed into the street.

Maddy scrambled out of bed and tiptoed downstairs. She did not want to wake her mother. On the counter, there was a plate of bagels and a jar of jam, with a note propped against it. *Maddy, please make breakfast for yourself and your mother. Toasted bagels with butter and jam. And a pot of tea. Thanks, Dan.*

Maddy sniffed. Hmm, that sounded like a friendlier Dan. She guessed he'd had a good sleep. She quickly buttered a bagel and bit into it. Then she pushed two more into a baggie and headed for the woodshed. But as soon as she climbed to the loft, her heart sank. Still no door in the back wall. She scanned the shadows for the cat. Why? Why didn't that cat show up when she needed her?

With a despairing sigh, Maddy shoved the bagels into her backpack. She'd eat them later on the train. If later actually happened. She reluctantly returned to the kitchen where she toasted a bagel for her mother. After spreading jam on it, she arranged the plate and cup of tea on a tray and carried them upstairs. Her mother was lying on the mattress, which had fallen to the floor below the bed frame. When she heard Maddy's quiet "Mom?" she opened her eyes and grinned.

"Dan says he'll fix it when he gets home." She pushed herself into a sitting position. "But I'll need help getting out of bed."

"Stay there, Mom!" Maddy nudged the tray onto the crowded dresser top. "You can have breakfast in bed."

When she tucked the blanket around her mother's legs

she accidently bumped her round belly. Carla winced.

"Oops! Did that hurt?"

"Things feel sore today," her mother replied with a rueful smile. Then she patted the bed and said, "Put the plate here. I'll drink my tea later."

As Carla slowly chewed her bagel, Maddy searched for a place to sit. Everything was covered with baby clothes and blankets. She squished herself next to a pile of diapers on the flowered armchair.

"When I was a baby inside you, were you always this tired? Did I make you sore too?"

Carla shook her head. "I was pretty young then, only twenty. And for some people, like me, having babies when you're a bit older is harder."

Apprehension prickled Maddy. "You going to be okay?"

"Don't worry, hon. I'll be fine." Carla held out the plate with an uneaten half bagel. "But that's all I can eat. Not much room in here for food." She patted her stomach. "Maybe you can help me organize this baby stuff after I shower?"

Maddy agreed. Despite her mother's reassurances, Maddy was worried about her. The circles under her eyes seemed darker and Maddy noticed that her mother's hands shook as she sipped her tea. Maddy felt torn. The baby clothes were cute. Pandas and teddy bears decorated the sleepers on the pile near her feet. The one with a rainbow reminded her of a favorite shirt she wore when she was four or five. Sorting through the clothes might be as fun as shopping for her own. But a big part of Maddy longed to head back to the loft in the woodshed and return to her mission in Clare and Eva's world. For a few moments, she fidgeted in her chair, wrestling with the urgent and competing demands of both times.

"Sweetie," Carla said softly. "You look so preoccupied. Anything the matter?"

Maddy blinked. There was lots the matter, no doubt about that, but nothing she could share with her mother.

"I'm afraid I've not paid much attention to you since we moved here. With all the unpacking . . . and the baby coming . . ."

"Don't worry, Mom. I'm fine." Maddy's foot began to tap on the floor. Except she needed to get out of here soon.

"Won't it be great to have a baby sister?" her mother asked, a wistful note creeping into her voice.

"Probably, Mom." Maddy avoided her gaze as she jumped up to place her empty teacup on the tray. Since she met Clare, she hadn't thought much about the baby's arrival. When her mother had first sheepishly broken the news about her pregnancy, Maddy didn't know how to feel about it. Excited, perhaps. There had been times when she had wished for a younger brother or sister. But her friend Amy had quashed that desire. Babies, as Amy had flatly stated, were a pain in the neck. She should know. Her own mother had three of them, all younger than five. There was lots of crying and tons of dirty diapers.

Carla had laughed when told about Amy's view of her siblings. "Not to worry, hon," she had reassured her daughter. "Nothing's really going to change here."

But of course, it had. Almost immediately. Within weeks, Dan had convinced Carla to abandon their cozy, modern bungalow in the city for a very odd antique house in the country. Then as her belly grew, her energy faded away. Often, she seemed spacey, lost in her own inner world. Lately

Maddy wondered if her old mom would ever return after the baby was born or if she was gone for good.

As Maddy helped her mother struggle over the bed frame and onto her feet, Carla reassured her that a hot shower would get her going.

"Be a sweetheart and check the mailbox. I'd love to see my last assignment in the new issue of *Country Crafts.*" Carla tugged a clean summer dress off its hanger and shuffled towards the bathroom.

When Maddy headed to the mailbox, the old woman from across the street was backing her car out of her driveway. She stopped it in the road.

"Hello, Maddy," she said as she rolled down the window. "How's your mother?"

"Fine," Maddy mumbled.

"Don't worry, dearie. All will be well." With a wave, the woman drove down the street.

Bewildered, Maddy shook her head. What was that about?

In the mailbox, on top of the magazine, lay a postcard from Amy. Its large, red letters, *Greetings From Loon Lake*, flashed above a sparkling northern lake that was bordered with tall pine trees. On the other side, in purple ink, Amy had scrawled, *See me on the beach? Getting a great tan! Lots of cute guys! LOL!* Maddy studied the tiny figures in the picture. Amy could be any one in the crowd. But, obviously, none were Maddy. She frowned. "Maybe," she muttered to herself, "I should have agreed to let Dan drive me up north. Nothing in my life seems to be working out right now."

As she trudged upstairs, she called, "Mom, here's your magazine. Look, I got a postcard from—" She stopped mid-sentence. Her mother was awkwardly climbing over the bed frame back into bed.

"What's the matter, Mom? Aren't you going to get dressed?"

Carla shook her wet head and sank into the mattress. "I'm exhausted. It's so hard to get a good night's sleep. I think I'll nap for a while." As she pulled the blanket to her chin, she added, "Please don't go away today."

Maddy nodded. Napping was a good idea, but still, something wasn't right. Why was her mother's face so pale? Was that normal? Maddy kissed her mother's forehead and promised to check up on her in an hour. But when she walked past the living room window, she saw a black tail disappear behind the lilac bush. Maddy paused mid-stride. When Shadow showed up, the portal into the attic was open. Excitement and a rush of relief sprang up inside Maddy. Despite her promise to remain home, she couldn't resist the pull into the past, nor the desire to get on with her plans. With only a moment's hesitation, she swung open the octagon's front door, dashed to the woodshed, and scrambled up its ladder.

Chapter 19

Standing in the long attic room, Maddy listened for sounds from below. All seemed quiet. She grabbed Eva's dress off the hook, quickly slipped it over her head, and buttoned its sleeves. Then she kicked off her running shoes and tugged on Eva's boots. She tied the ribbon from the straw hat around her neck so that it fell onto her back. After tucking the pills and her two-dollar bill into a side pocket in backpack, she slung it over her shoulder. She was ready to go. All she had to do was find Clare and convince him to temporarily abandon their soap project and buy two train tickets to Belleville. They could wrap and sell the soap later. Then when Eva was feeling better, Clare could send her a ticket to visit him. Why hadn't she thought of this plan before? She smiled at the thought of all three of them hanging out together in the barn.

Heart racing, Maddy climbed down the steep steps to the narrow, green door. Her backpack bumped it open without a sound. She slipped past the porcelain sink to the kitchen door. As her hand lifted its latch, she heard a man's voice cry "Amen."

Maddy stopped. From the parlor in the octagon came the sound of chairs scraping the floor. Other voices began to sing, first the women's high notes and then the deep rumble of men joining the slow rhythm of the song—"O God, our help in ages past, our hope for years to come." Maddy peered cautiously into the kitchen. Across the room, she glimpsed the long black skirts of women crowding the small triangular hallway that lead to the octagon's parlor.

Maddy jerked her head back into the creamery. What was going on? She had expected to see Aunt Ella. Maybe even Clare. But a room full of people all dressed in black? Shivers shot up her back. She closed the door quietly and spun on her heels towards the attic stairs; it would be easier to observe everything through the floor grate up there.

Then she noticed the open creamery window. The wooden box was still on the ground below it. She hitched up her dress, crawled over the windowsill, and jumped down.

Maddy peeked around the back wall of the kitchen, hoping to see what was going on through the living room window, but light reflecting off the glass obscured her view. The impatient stamping of hooves caught her attention. In front of the house, a horse with long, white ribbons strung in its halter waited in the road. Behind it stood a rough-hewn wagon, a wide black cloth draped along its sides.

With a rusty moan, the narrow door at the side of the octagon swung open. Uncle Ray, wearing a long black coat, backed through the opening. Bent over he gripped the handle of a wooden box. His feet shuffled slowly, searching for the cement step down to the grass. A man, clean-shaven, also dressed in black, emerged holding the other end of the box. Behind him stumbled Clare, his pale face taut with sadness. He clutched a small, cedar wreath with a white ribbon laced through its branches.

The men carried the box to the wagon, carefully placed it on the back, and pushed it forward. Clare climbed onto the seat behind the horse and slid the wreath on top of the box. Gripping its side, Uncle Ray mounted the wagon. He picked up the horse's reins and waited silently with Clare. Both stared straight ahead.

As clouds gathered overhead, Maddy huddled against the wall of the house. The box in the wagon was a coffin. She knew that. Not as polished as Grammy Bea's, but a coffin nonetheless. Dread, like the cold beneath her feet, rose to envelop her. She began to shiver. It was only yesterday that that she had left Clare at the mill. Everything had been fine. But now he looked so sad. Maddy tried to swallow the ache swelling in her throat, the horrid suspicion that was knotting her stomach. She peered around the corner at Clare. His blank, unsmiling face had not changed. Even though her knees felt like rubber, she wanted to run to the wagon and shout, *Clare, what happened?* She didn't care if Uncle Ray saw her. She needed an answer. She desperately wanted Clare to tell her that she was wrong. That she wasn't too late. That it wasn't Eva in that coffin behind him.

A large bush with long, arching branches grew close to the road where the wagon stood. Just as she started towards it, Uncle Ray picked up the horse's reins, slapped its rump, and steered the wagon onto the road.

Maddy sank to the ground and watched numbly as more

vehicles rolled into view. In a small, open buggy, she recognized Aunt Helen sitting upright and solemn on its wooden seat. Against her slumped a veiled woman wearing a hat decorated with a single black feather and a long black bow. Somehow Maddy knew that she was Clare's mother. Eva's mother. Then a surrey with a black fringed top lurched onto the road. Inside were four more adults and two children, all dressed in black. Two other wagons joined the procession that rolled slowly down the road and out of sight.

As the groan of wooden wheels faded away, Maddy sprang up and paced back and forth behind the house, swiping at the stalks of brown grass, her breath coming in short and shallow gasps. A few leaves tinged yellow and orange floated down from the maple tree. Maddy guessed that it was no longer the height of summer as it had been when she and Clare had poured the lavender soap into molds.

How much time had really passed since that day in the mill? Was their soap still hardening or had Clare sold it? Did it matter? If Eva had died, their project was over no matter where the bars lay.

A cool breeze blew from the creek and more dark clouds piled up to cover the bleak sun. Maddy rubbed her arms for warmth. She remembered that her sweatshirt was in her backpack, which she'd left on the creamery floor. And so was her puffer. She needed it to fill her lungs and ease the ache in her heart. As she stumbled towards the window, a black, whiskered face poked out and meowed loudly.

"Shadow!"

The cat meowed again and dropped into the house. Maddy climbed over the windowsill and reached to pet the cat, but Shadow backed away and meowed even louder.

Suddenly the creamery door burst open.

"You got a mouse, Shadow?" Aunt Ella demanded. When she saw Maddy, her hands flew to her chest and she reeled backwards.

"Eva!" She inhaled sharply, her face turning pale. Then she relaxed. "Maddy, you frightened me near to death. Why are you wearing the poor child's clothes?"

Maddy gulped. Her face reddened.

"Uh . . . uh . . ." Maddy looked down at the dress and smoothed its skirt. How could she explain things to Aunt Ella? The soap project . . . the pills . . . the train tickets? All she managed was a whispered "sorry" as she hung her head.

For a moment, Aunt Ella was silent. Then she solemnly said, "No matter. Eva won't be needing them now. The angels have taken her home."

Maddy's shoulders slumped and tears pooled in her eyes. She stared at her boots, Eva's boots. A wave of confusion and sadness washed over her. She had to get out of Eva's clothes. It was too weird to be wearing them. But when she turned towards the attic stairs, Aunt Ella reached out and touched her arm.

"Come, child. Have a cup of tea before the others return."

Maddy shook her head. "I shouldn't be here now, Aunt Ella." She turned towards the stairs, but the cat blocked her way with a plaintive "Meow." Then it marched into the kitchen.

Chapter 20

Maddy reluctantly followed Shadow and Aunt Ella into the kitchen. At the back of the cookstove, steam rose from the large, iron kettle. Beyond, on a lace-covered tablecloth, stacks of matching cups and saucers gathered around the china teapot with its delicate pattern of apple blossoms. Plates of food crowded the middle of the table—a loaf of bread, two cheeses, finger biscuits, a bowl of pickles, a round cake decorated with baked purple fruit.

"Aunt Ella," said Maddy in a subdued voice. "I don't like tea."

The old woman limped to the table, her hand rubbing her lower back. "Aye child, but you must eat something to keep up your spirits." She cut a large piece of cake and handed it to Maddy.

"'Tis plum cake. Eva's favorite."

The cake's spongy softness smelled wonderful. Even though she had no appetite, Maddy thought she could manage a few bites. She reached for a fork and sat down while Aunt Ella lowered herself into the rocking chair. From her knitting basket, the old woman pulled out a blue sweater.

"'Twas for Eva. For her stay in the mountains." She withdrew a white handkerchief from her sleeve and wiped her nose. "It's awhile since you've been here, child. Though I saw you once bounding down the stairs to the front door. But no matter."

Maddy's fork stopped halfway to her mouth. Aunt Ella had seen her running up and down the stairs? Well, that didn't seem so strange anymore. Maddy wondered what else the old woman had seen.

"The collar," Aunt Ella said as she picked a small knitted piece from her basket. "For Eva to fasten 'round her neck." She smoothed it on her lap, shaking her head. "Poor child. She never made it out of her house."

The cake stuck in Maddy's throat. With effort, she swallowed it and then pushed the plate onto the table behind her.

"What happened?" she asked.

Aunt Ella adjusted her glasses. "It was so sudden. A shock to us all." She wiped her nose again with the handkerchief. Maddy twisted her hands in her lap as she waited for Aunt Ella's story, anxious yet dreading to hear it.

"Four days ago," Aunt Ella began, "my niece Martha, Eva's mother, packed their trunks for the boat trip 'cross Lake Ontario to Oswego. There they were to stay at our cousin's house for a day of rest. After that, they planned to take the train to Saratoga where there's a famous doctor who has a clinic for people with consumption. They had in mind to board at a private home while Eva took the Cure for her condition."

Aunt Ella patted the collar piece on her lap and shifted it close to the neck of the sweater.

"On the day before they left, Eva complained of great tiredness. It weren't strange for the girl to nap in the afternoon. But later she had no appetite for her supper and begged to go to bed before dark. Martha finished her packing and retired early too. But in the middle of the night, she woke to Eva's coughing. She waited for it to stop, like it did most nights. But this time, Martha said it grew worse and worse until Eva cried out for her."

Aunt Ella paused and twisted the collar's button between her trembling fingers.

"Then what happened?" Maddy whispered.

"As quick as could be, Martha ran to Eva's side. The girl was struggling to sit up. Martha said her eyes were full of fright and that she kept coughing and coughing. It wouldn't stop and then blood rushed from her mouth. Like water from a bucket. Martha didn't know what to do. When it finally stopped, the poor child sank back on her pillow, and that was it. She was gone."

Aunt Ella patted the blue sweater and added softly, "Martha brought her here to be buried in our family plot not far from the lake." Then she looked up. The lines on her worn face pulled at her cheeks, showing great weariness. Sorrow filled her eyes. She sighed deeply, shook her head, and said in a voice Maddy strained to hear, "A terrible thing it is when your child dies."

For a very long moment, silence filled the room. Only the ticking of the silver clock from the living room could be heard in the kitchen. Maddy sat motionless in her chair watching Aunt Ella fold and refold the blue sweater on her lap. While the old woman tucked it into her knitting bag, Maddy glanced down at her own hands gripping the folds of Eva's dress. She winced. She suddenly understood that she shouldn't be wearing it. She felt like a little child playing a dress-up game, and it was too much for a day when everyone was wearing black and no one was smiling, not even Aunt Ella who kept wiping her nose with a handkerchief.

The air in the kitchen hung heavy with sadness and the overwhelmingly sweet scent of flowers and perfumed cakes. All at once, Maddy began to tremble. She felt very out of place. She didn't belong here. Her throat tightened more. She couldn't breathe. She stood abruptly and darted across the kitchen floor towards the creamery.

"Wait, child!" Aunt Ella called after her. "Give me a hand with the kettle. They'll be wanting their tea soon."

Maddy wanted nothing more than to escape the grief of that day and her intrusion into it. She needed air! She didn't care about the tea. But she knew the iron kettle was heavy. She turned back, lifted it with both hands, and carefully filled the teapot to the top. This time, not a drop fell on the stove. Aunt Ella shuffled towards her and patted her arm.

"Thanks, dearie. You've been a big help."

Outside, wagon wheels creaked on the driveway.

"Whoa!" Uncle Ray's voice rang out. "Clare, take the horse and wagon to the barn."

Chapter 21

When Maddy heard Clare's name, she realized she couldn't just leave. She had to see him, even though she wasn't sure why. Even though her lungs ached for air and she should be pulling her puffer out of her backpack and using it. But she had to act fast.

Without a goodbye to Aunt Ella, she dashed up the stairs to the attic, scooped her clothes off the floor, and bolted down to the creamery. Then she snatched her backpack and climbed out the window. As she rounded the corner of the drive shed, she stopped abruptly. Uncle Ray, his back to her, was striding towards a buggy turning into the driveway. So no one would see her, she ran around the chicken coop and slipped through the barn doors.

Inside, head bent down, Clare was halting the horse and wagon with a quiet "Whoa, boy." He patted the horse's back and glanced up at the doorway where Maddy stood in the shadows. He gasped and stumbled backwards. The horse whinnied and veered away.

"Clare, it's me, Maddy!"

He stared at her, frozen and wide-eyed. Finally, he stammered, "I thought you was . . ." Then he mumbled wearily, "You're too late." His eyes, too, were full of sorrow.

A sharp pain pierced Maddy's heart. She longed to tell him why she was wearing Eva's dress, but her plans no longer mattered. Instead she held up her own clothes and headed towards the storage room. There, she dug out her puffer, inhaled, held her breath until she felt a tingle, and slowly exhaled. The bitter taste of Ventolin filled her mouth. Why hadn't she packed her water bottle? But that really didn't matter. She was having an asthma attack, and as hard as it was to breathe, she knew she'd get past it. Maddy shuddered, remembering the description of Eva's last breaths. That poor girl had suffered from far worse than asthma. Maddy would live. She had her puffer. She knew how to calm herself and control the attacks. She even had stronger medication if she needed it. If only, she agonized, she hadn't been too late getting the antibiotics to Eva.

With that grim thought, Maddy tucked her puffer into her backpack and the pills next to it. She carefully folded Eva's dress and placed it on a wooden box. When she finally reemerged from the storage room wearing her jeans and T-shirt, Clare had unhitched the horse from the wagon and tethered it in its stall. Maddy watched him for a minute. He was so quiet, so withdrawn. She didn't know what to say. She had no words for the confusion of sorrow and guilt inside her.

"Want me to feed it some oats?" she finally asked.

He nodded without looking at her. She scooped grain from a bin and dumped it into the horse's feedbox. Uncertain of what to do next, she watched as he brushed the horse.

When Clare began to untie the white ribbons from its halter, she stepped forward to help. Together they undid the knots. Out of the corner of her eye, Maddy watched the muscles on his forearms flex and relax. Maddy wanted to touch them, to somehow tell him how badly she felt that Eva had died. But she couldn't. He seemed so far away, and she felt too uncertain.

He looked up and held out his hand for the ribbons. Their eyes met for a second. Then he backed away, shoving the ribbons in his pocket. With a slight jerk of his head, he pointed at the wagon and the long, black cloth that decorated its sides.

"I need your help folding the bunting." His voice was barely audible. "Aunt Ella wants it done properly, without wrinkles."

They each unfastened an end of the long cloth and held it straight and taut between them. As they folded it and walked its corners close together, Clare's fingers brushed hers and she nearly let go of her end. With an awkward thrust, she pushed it at him. His mouth twitched and the grimness in his face softened. Maddy dropped her eyes. She felt her face redden.

"Guess I'll go back now," she said, rubbing her hands on her jeans. But when he mumbled "wait a bit" and began to maneuver the wagon into the corner of the barn, she scrambled over the hitch and helped rock it into place.

Not able to contain her feelings any longer, she blurted, "Clare, it's all my fault. I should have gotten those pills to her sooner. They could have saved her life. But the door to the attic disappeared, and the cat wouldn't show up, and then too much time passed . . . Oh, Clare, I'm so sorry."

"It wasn't your fault she got sick, Maddy. And it wasn't your fault she died." Clare's face hardened. "Dying just happens. It can't be stopped. If God wants to take someone Home, then that's what happens. We die and there's nothing you can do about it."

"That's not true," Maddy said. "Antibiotics cure lots of people. Like me . . . from bronchitis. I had it real bad! And antibiotics cured my Grammy Bea from pneumonia!"

For a moment Clare stared at the rafters high above and said nothing. Then he lowered his gaze directly at Maddy and shook his head. "That medicine ain't a part of our world, Maddy."

"Not true," she said fiercely as she reached into her backpack and pulled out the pills. "They're right here."

"Aye, but they didn't change a thing, did they?"

Maddy shook her head ever so slightly. No. No, they did not. She shoved them into her pocket. She felt bitter. She had tried so hard to help Eva. She had faith those pills would somehow cure her. And now Clare had said they didn't belong in their world. That dying just happens and nothing can be done about it. Well, maybe that was true about old people like her grandmother. But Eva was so young, just a year or two older than herself. She should have had a chance to get better. She should have been spared from that horrible disease.

For a long moment all was quiet in the barn. Clare turned and picked up a currycomb. Maddy watched him brush the horse with swift strokes along its back.

Finally, she asked in a small voice mixed with sad resignation "Clare, what will we do with our soap?"

To her astonishment, Clare threw up his hands. The comb dropped to the floor. "I don't care about that soap! Nobody's going to buy it." He stared at her, sparks of anger flashing in his eyes.

Maddy stepped back, bewildered by his reaction. Clare had never said anything unkind to her before, even when she had fumbled stirring the soap in the factory and he had cut his finger.

"But that's not true," she protested.

Clare's eyes narrowed. "Your grand ideas don't work out, Maddy! I never believed that making fancy soap could make a difference. But you was so excited up there in the mansion, I decided to go along with your plans. Anything to help Eva get better. When those little soaps turned out so sweet-smelling, I thought maybe they'd sell real fast and we'd be able to . . ." He searched for words. "But then you never showed up like you promised and now those fancy soaps just sit in the mill gathering dust, like all the other soap."

"Clare . . . the cat . . ."

"Shadow don't make a difference. She ain't a door-keeper. For all I know, you don't live anywhere near here. You just show up when you want to. When you got nothing better to do with your yourself." He lowered his voice. "Or when Dan's bothering you too much."

Maddy gasped. Tears sprang into her eyes. She felt as if she had been slapped. For a moment she stared at her feet, and then, shoulders stiff, she picked up her backpack. Maybe there was truth in what Clare had said. Maybe she was escaping her unhappiness when she followed Shadow into the past. But accusing her of lying about the cat and where she came from? That wasn't fair. And, she certainly hadn't meant to meddle in his life or anyone else's. She'd only wanted to help Clare and Eva. Well, it hadn't worked out. Eva was gone. And their soap project was abandoned in the mill. It was obvious Clare was fed up with the whole thing . . . and with her too.

She headed to the barn door.

"Wait," Clare called after her. Maddy paused. She turned to face him and saw that his whole self—his arms, his shoulders, his eyes—drooped with exhaustion.

"It ain't right for me to yell at you, Maddy," he said, the anger fading from his face. "But I believe you need to go back to your own people and sort things out there."

Images of Carla's weary face and Dan's stern eyes arose in Maddy's mind. She nodded—Clare was probably right. Without a reply, she stepped into the chilly afternoon air. A cold wind rushed at her, scattering brown leaves around her feet. Maddy hunched her shoulders and hurried past the chicken coop and the drive shed to the back of the house. The creamery window was open. Voices from the kitchen rose above the clink of forks on china plates. Maddy climbed inside the house and pulled her backpack after her, dislodging the board propping up the window. It fell with a loud thud. The voices stopped abruptly. Not hesitating, Maddy scrambled up the stairs into the attic and through the small door to the loft in her own world.

Chapter 22

Out of breath, Maddy collapsed onto the captain's chair in the woodshed and gulped its dry, stale air until her heartbeat slowed. A dim light filtered through the dusty window. Was it morning? Late afternoon? Maddy had lost all track of time. She vaguely remembered leaving the attic full of hope, with the pills and the two-dollar bill for train fare. But now . . . here she was again, back in the loft of her own time, and Eva was dead. Even buried. And Clare was heartbroken and angry at her for raising his expectations of curing Eva with those pills. Maddy fished for them in her backpack. She had a strong urge to grind them on the floor with her foot, but instead tugged up the loft's rickety window and threw them into the long weeds below where she hoped they'd dissolve in the rain that was threatening to fall from the black clouds gathering overhead.

Then she heard the rumble of a truck starting up. It shifted into forward gear and raced away. From somewhere below, a voice called her name. Poppa George? A second later, she heard it again. The voice sounded worried. Maddy hesitated, but when she heard her name a third time, she leapt towards the ladder. In her haste, she missed a rung and scraped her leg on its rough surface.

"There you are!" her grandfather said as she limped into the kitchen. "I've been looking all over for you." His gaze shifted to her leg. "You're bleeding!"

Maddy glanced down at her leg where a rip in her jeans revealed red scratches and then, around the kitchen. It was so quiet, so still. No Aunt Ella. No table piled high with food. No one eating plum cake on china plates after Eva's funeral.

"Sit down, Maddy." Poppa George waved his hand at a chair. "I'll get something for that cut."

In a daze, Maddy heard him open the cupboard door in the bathroom and return with a box of Band-Aids. She took one.

"Why are you here?" she finally asked, rubbing her fingers on the smooth paper of the Band-Aid, in no hurry to open it.

"I just got back from Kingston."

"Where is everybody?"

Poppa George lowered himself into the rocking chair and wiped his forehead with a handkerchief from his pocket.

"Dan's driving your mother to the hospital."

In a second, Maddy's confusion with time and place drained out of her, leaving a dank puddle of worry in the pit of her stomach.

"What's wrong with Mom?" The Band-Aid fluttered to

the floor.

"We don't know, hon. She lay down for a nap this morning. When Dan came home, he found her curled up in bed. Seems she had bad cramps and started to bleed."

Maddy sank into a chair, sharp remorse and a flood of fear rising inside her. She shouldn't have followed Shadow. She shouldn't have left her mother alone. Nothing good had come out of it. Not in the past. Not now.

"Poppa," Maddy whispered. "Is something wrong with the baby?"

"I don't know, hon. But don't you worry. They'll take good care of your mother at the hospital."

For a moment, Maddy was lost in darker and darker thoughts that whirled around her. Then she burst out, "Is the baby going to be born now?" She didn't dare voice her fear of her unborn sister dying before she even took her first breath.

"Let's hope not, Maddy." Poppa George gave her a tired smile. "It's a little too soon for that." He drummed his fingers on the arm of the rocking chair and then exclaimed with forced enthusiasm, "Best not to sit here and worry. Let's make supper!"

"I'm not hungry, Poppa." The thought of food made Maddy's stomach churn even more. But when her grandfather heaved himself out of the rocker, she reluctantly agreed to pick beans in the garden before the rain started. At first, she couldn't find them because the beds were overgrown with weeds. She felt guilty that she hadn't helped her mother pull them out long ago. When Maddy finally discovered the beans under run-away squash vines, she filled the basket with all the green and yellow ones she could find, hoping her mother would come home soon and be pleased she had picked them all.

For supper, Maddy and her grandfather silently ate steamed beans with tuna fish on toast. Every few minutes, they glanced at the phone on the wall. Long after their dishes were loaded into the dishwasher, when the sun had sunk behind the sumacs, Dan finally called.

"Hmm," Poppa George exhaled after listening to Dan's brief message. "Don't worry about us, son. Just call back when you can." He hung up the phone.

"Well?"

"Seems it's complicated, hon. The bleeding stopped. But they're moving Carla to a hospital in Toronto where they can monitor her better. She needs total bed rest so the baby can grow inside her for as long as possible."

"Can't she rest here? I promise I'll take good care of her."

"If the bleeding starts again, she might need an emergency cesarean."

"A what?"

"An operation, hon, where they take the baby out through the mother's abdomen."

Maddy gasped. That sounded super scary. A tear slid down her cheek. Then another. Things were getting worse and it was all her fault. First Eva's death. Then Clare's deep sadness and his unexpected anger towards her. And now, maybe, the baby's early birth. A numbing exhaustion swept over Maddy. It was too much. She wanted to run away. Or at the very least, be alone.

She sprang out of her chair.

"I'm going to bed!"

Poppa George reached to hug her. "Don't worry so

much, Maddy. Your mom will be fine." She rested her head against his chest and relaxed for a moment. But dread had a tighter grip on her. With a despairing sigh, she wriggled out of his embrace and dragged herself upstairs.

In her darkened bedroom, Maddy tossed her backpack into the corner and sank on her knees in front of the window, resting her arms on its sill. Outside, across the driveway, uncut grass waved in the breeze. As Maddy stared across its expanse, she could almost see the red barn and, next to it, the chicken coop. That afternoon, when she had left the barn, hens had been scratching in the dirt. She wondered if Eva's chick was alive and part of the flock. She felt keenly how unfair it was that Eva could no longer feed it or collect its eggs. Again, sharp remorse stabbed at her heart. If only she hadn't failed in getting those pills to her.

Then out of the night's gathering darkness, Clare's insistent words, *That medicine ain't part of our world*, echoed in her head. As if the rising moon was shining right through her window and shedding light on her memory, Maddy saw forgotten words on the library's computer screen. Words she had skimmed over quickly and ignored. Words that said antibiotics to cure tuberculosis hadn't been developed until the 1950s. That was decades after Eva had died! Maybe, Maddy reasoned, that was what Clare had meant. Maybe, somehow, Clare knew that something not available in his and Eva's time had no capability of changing their lives. Perhaps, no matter how powerful the pills were in her time, they could not cure the illnesses of the past. In an odd way, that thought gave Maddy a sense of relief. Maybe it really wasn't her fault that Eva had died, for there was nothing she could ever have done to change her death. It had happened way before she was even born.

But then another thought crowded into her head. If she hadn't convinced Clare to make their lavender soap, his hopes for curing Eva wouldn't have been raised. And then dashed when she died. She really had meddled in his life.

"Ohhh," Maddy groaned and held her head between her hands. She wanted to cry, but tears still would not come. Clare's voice echoed again in her head—*You need to go back to your own people and sort things out there.* She cringed at the memory. Not only had she interfered in his life—and disappointed him big time—but she had done so when she should have been paying more attention to her own world. If she had stayed home instead of running after Shadow, she would have checked up on her mother as she had promised. She would have realized something was wrong. She would have called Dan and he would have rushed home. Instead her mother waited hours for him to show up. And now maybe it was too late . . .

Maddy shuddered, buried her head in her arms, and sobbed. She had failed everyone. Her mother. Clare. Even Dan. She'd made promises she hadn't kept. Poked her nose into other people's lives. Ignored her own family. What kind of daughter was she? What kind of friend?

When Maddy finally lifted her wet face and stared across the driveway, everything was pitch black outside. Clouds covered the moon and the darkness reached inside and filled her heart. Exhausted and drained, she crawled into bed and pulled the covers over her head.

All night she dreamed of stumbling through a huge vegetable garden. Sometimes she glimpsed her mother's face, sometimes Clare's, even once Dan's, emerging above the overgrown tomato and zucchini plants, calling to her. But every time she reached out to them, a vine wrapped itself around her and pulled her down into the weeds.

Chapter 23

The next morning, Maddy woke, tangled in her sheets and as exhausted as she had been before she fell asleep. Outside her window, a cardinal's whistle chided her, *Do something, do something.* Maddy pushed herself upright. Her limbs felt like lead, unable to move on their own accord.

But do what?

Maddy rubbed her forehead trying to clear the muddle inside. After a few moments, the answer seemed simple. She needed to find Clare. He was her friend and it was time to apologize. Time to tell him how sorry she felt that things hadn't worked out. That she had truly wanted to help Eva because she cared about her and about Clare too.

But nagging doubts kept Maddy from getting out of bed. What if Clare didn't want to see her? What if he would have none of her apology? And what about her mother, who was still in the hospital, maybe still in danger of something going wrong?

Outside, the cardinal chided her again, *Do Something!* It's shrill whistle, louder than before, jolted her out of her uncertainty. She would find Clare. After all, there wasn't much she could do about her mother, who was being looked after by nurses and doctors. But she wouldn't stay long, not more than an hour or two. With that promise to herself, she jumped up and tugged on her jeans

Standing on the front porch, Maddy glimpsed a flash of red feathers fly from the maple tree towards the back of the house. She hurried up the driveway, swung open the heavy woodshed door, and climbed the ladder to the loft.

From the corner, Shadow sprang towards her. Maddy stifled a scream. Tail held high, the cat scooted through the small door into the attic room. In a flash, Shadow bounded down the stairs and through the creamery, with Maddy trailing behind her. In the kitchen, Aunt Ella sat knitting in her rocking chair. She nodded at Maddy and pointed with a needle towards the open door.

"He'll be in the mill today," she said.

Maddy hurried outside towards the large wooden building across the street. When she peered into its dark interior, Clare was lifting a wooden crate onto the drying racks. Unsure what to say or do, she watched him pack bars of soap until a gust of wind banged the mill door against the building. Clare glanced up at the sound and stared at her for a moment.

Finally he said, "Careful on the slipp'ry floor."

The corners of Maddy's mouth turned up in a small smile that she knew he couldn't see from across the room.

"No worries," she replied as she carefully made her way

towards him. When she reached the huge tub in the middle of the room, she hesitated. Clare continued to place the large yellow bars into the crate, one at a time.

"Getting ready to make deliveries in town?"

"Nope," he said in his matter-of-fact voice, pulling more bars towards him. "Uncle Ray plans to sell the mill. I'm packing all our supplies for some guy in the next town over."

"What! Your uncle's selling the mill?"

"It ain't making money. No one wants to buy his soap. He's talking to the lawyer, firming up his plans."

Maddy longed to ask Clare about their lavender soap but remembered too clearly his reaction in the barn. As if sensing her thoughts, Clare pointed to the shelf next to her and said, "I put our little soaps in that box where you're standing."

Maddy reached into it and ran her finger over the soaps' smooth surfaces. She chose a small one and held it to her nose, sniffing its floral scent.

"People would buy this lavender soap," she said quietly, but without hesitation.

"Don't matter now." Clare slid an empty crate next to his full one. "Mother wants to move to Toronto. Take me with her."

Maddy stared at Clare with dismay. "Really?"

"She can get good wages making hats for rich city ladies. She also knows a grocer looking for a boy to run his errands."

A lump rose in Maddy's throat. She hated the thought of Clare moving away and never seeing him again, even though he had almost told her flat out that she should focus on her own family rather than his. But she still wanted to somehow remain his friend and spend time together. Instinctively, she knew she had to tell him right away.

"Clare," she began, holding the little bar of soap tightly in her hand. "You were right about a lot of those things you said in the barn. Sometimes when I showed up in your life, I was running away from my own problems. I guess I should have been fixing them instead of interfering in yours. Maybe I shouldn't be here now because things aren't working out at home, but that isn't what I want to tell you."

Clare kept his head bent while he loaded more bars into the second crate, but Maddy could tell he was listening to her by how quietly he worked. She took a deep breath and rushed on.

"You might not believe that Shadow somehow opens that door in the attic, but you should know that when she does, I love going through it and hanging out with you and doing things together. You know, I only saw Eva once—that day when I peeked through the grate in the floor after I found the attic. I never met her, but I truly wanted to help her because you became my friend and Eva seemed so special to you. But I guess I had no business trying to convince you those pills would cure her. Maybe they could have, but maybe not either. You may be right about them not being part of your world."

Maddy paused and then added in a subdued voice, "I think I should have just helped you find a way to visit your sister more often."

Clare raised his head and looked at Maddy, his eyes again full of sadness.

"You know, Maddy, I never did see Eva again. I never

had a chance to say goodbye, she went so fast."

Tears welled up in his eyes and he brushed them away.

Maddy's eyes too were moist.

"Clare," she said softly. "I'm truly sorry."

He sighed deeply but said nothing. After a moment, Maddy replaced the lavender bar next to the others in the box and pushed it away. She hadn't a clue what to do or say next. Were there any words that could make up for her blundering or help him feel better?

Unexpectedly, Clare stepped alongside her and said in a quiet voice, "They're real pretty, aren't they?"

Maddy traced her fingertip over the edge of the box.

"I still think folks would buy our soap," she said softly.

"I have an idea in mind," he replied, a faraway look in his eye. "When we buried Eva, there was a gravestone in the cemetery with an angel on it. Not a big one, but it had a kindly face that seemed to be watching over the grave. Do you think . . ." His voice trailed away.

"I do!" Maddy said. "If our soap sells, you should buy Eva an angel!"

"She would like that." Clare smiled at her, a glimmer of light rising in his eyes. "Would you wrap them up like we planned? Mrs. Robinson at the Colebrook Store could display them on her shelves."

Maddy immediately agreed. She felt grateful to have a new plan, one that might lessen Clare's pain and make things right between them, one that he had proposed instead of her. She told him where to find the wrapping paper and ribbon in the attic. Before he went to retrieve them, he handed her a cloth to smooth the edges of the bars. After he returned, he took over her job and she wrapped each soap in tissue paper and tied it with a purple ribbon. Then Clare placed the little packages into a shallow crate to protect the paper from wrinkling.

"They look lovely!" Maddy said.

Clare counted the bars. Two dozen. He frowned.

"That may not be enough for an angel."

"How much do angels cost?"

"I don't know. But bars of soap are cheap. Twenty-four of them, fancy or not, won't get us far."

"I've got money, Clare! A two-dollar bill from your time! Poppa George . . ."

Suddenly Maddy remembered she had left the house early that morning before her grandfather had woken up. She felt uneasy. She sensed something wasn't right at home, maybe with her mother. She was sure that Poppa George was looking for her.

"Clare! I can't stay! I've got to get back home . . . to our house. I mean my house." Clare looked confused, but Maddy couldn't explain again how his house and her house, the one right across the street, were the same house but a century apart. She couldn't convince him that she truly didn't live in his time because she didn't understand it herself. But she did know that it was urgent she left his world right away.

"The money's in my backpack! Somewhere. I'll find it and come back as soon as I can." With those words as a goodbye, Maddy flew out of the barn and down the driveway to the attic that led to the loft that led to Maddy's present life and more complications.

Chapter 24

When Maddy tiptoed into the kitchen, Poppa George was scooping coffee beans into the grinder. The worry lines on his face looked deeper than the night before. He didn't smile when he saw her. Maddy was searching for an explanation as to why she hadn't been sleeping in her bedroom when he blurted, "Gotta get moving, Maddy. Dan just called."

"What?"

"Don't worry. Carla's doing fine. And your sister too."

"My sister?"

As Poppa George poured water into the coffee maker, he explained that her sister had been born just after midnight by cesarean section. She was tiny and was having a hard time breathing, so they had whisked her away to a special, neonatal nursery for premature babies.

"But don't worry," her grandfather repeated, frowning

into his empty coffee cup.

Why did grownups always say not to worry when worry was exactly what they were doing? Just as she feared, something must really be wrong. Images of her mother and her baby sister tumbled inside her head like clothes in a dryer. Jitters took hold of her body. She stumbled to her room to change into a clean top and jeans. For good measure, she quickly inhaled from her puffer and tucked it into her pocket.

Less than a half hour later, Maddy pulled the seat belt around her body. Her knees gripped a vase of flowers picked from her mother's garden. Zinnias. Calendulas. Cosmos.

Poppa George was such a pokey driver. As he drove along country roads towards the city, she wondered why they couldn't just take the highway. They would never get to the hospital at this rate. Ahead of them, lights began to flash at the railroad crossing. Poppa George slowed to a stop. A passenger train whizzed past. In the last car, a boy's face pressed against the window. His flat cap was pulled low on his forehead. Maddy thought of Clare and the puzzled expression on his face as she dashed out of the mill that morning. She wished she could tell him about the flowers she had picked for her mother and her trip to Toronto to see her new baby sister. Then he might smile his approval, but he'd probably just nod and get back to work without comment because, in his life, doing what you were supposed to do was its own reward.

Suddenly, the car began to roll forward and bump over the tracks. Water from the vase splashed Maddy's jeans. She watched the wet spot spread over her leg. Great!

Now she looked like she had peed herself. She

desperately hoped things were going to get better that day.

Two towns later, where the countryside gave way to industrial buildings and shopping malls, Poppa George pulled onto the highway. Soon three lanes turned into four and then to express lanes and finally to the parkway heading south into the heart of the city. Maddy gritted her teeth as cars raced past. A driver honked his horn and gestured for Poppa George to move over. At last, he exited onto the ramp that funneled them to city streets where all traffic slowed to a crawl. After waiting at countless red lights, they drove into an underground parking lot by the hospital where Poppa slowly backed into a parking space.

Maddy hesitated to open the car door. Her chest tightened. Her knees felt weak. She sensed it wasn't from the car ride. She desperately hoped her mother would look normal. Not so pale. No dark circles under her eyes. In the elevator Maddy whispered under her breath, "Please Dan, don't be there." She was certain he blamed her for causing all this trouble.

On the third floor, outside Room 305, Poppa George silently nodded at the coffee machine down the hall while he held the door open for Maddy. She stepped inside the darkened room. From the doorway, she could only see her mother's feet covered by a white cotton blanket. They didn't move.

"Mom?" she whispered, tiptoeing towards the bed. Carla lay on her back, her long hair fanned around her head. At the sound of Maddy's voice, her eyes fluttered open. She struggled to sit up, winced, and sank back into her pillows. Maddy thrust the flowers towards her.

"From your garden, Mom."

Carla smiled weakly and waved a finger at the tray stand. Maddy placed the vase next to a glass with a bendy straw. Then she leaned against the bed.

"Careful," her mother grimaced and pointed at her stomach.

"Does it hurt?"

"Only when I move."

Maddy imagined that was probably all the time and stared at the floor, willing herself not to cry.

"I'm sorry," she said.

Carla rested a hand on Maddy's arm.

"You have a baby sister, hon."

"I know. Poppa told me."

At the sound of his name, Poppa George stepped forward, a cup of coffee in hand, and beamed at his daughter.

"You look lovely, Carla!"

"Hardly," she said with a rueful smile.

True. There were still dark circles under her eyes. And they looked puffy, like she'd been crying.

"Where's the baby?" asked Maddy.

"Upstairs, in the intensive care nursery." Her mother's smile faded. "Dan and I went to see her this morning. He's still there, just watching her. She's so tiny." Tears filled her eyes.

Maddy bent forward and rested her head on her mother's shoulder. She felt terrible, afraid that her inattentiveness had caused her mother's pain and this whole awful mess. While Carla lightly stroked her hair, Maddy pressed a little closer. Her mother's lips brushed her cheeks. They both closed their eyes and rested together for a few minutes until Maddy felt Poppa George's hand on her shoulder.

"Best let your mom sleep now, Maddy. Let's go to the nursery to see your sister."

Maddy reluctantly pushed herself up. "Right now?"

"Sure. Dan might like company."

"He won't like my company."

"It's all right, hon," her mother said, eyes still closed. "He's tired, not upset with you."

"Yeah, sure. He's always upset with me."

"Not really, Maddy. Just concerned."

Concerned? About what? Was there something her mother wasn't telling her? Maddy was too afraid to ask. Instead, she tucked the blanket around her mother's shoulders and kissed her forehead.

"Sleep tight, Mom." she said.

Chapter 25

When the elevator door opened on the hospital's seventh floor, Poppa George gave Maddy's shoulder a squeeze.

"Hang in there, Maddy. You'll be fine."

Maddy frowned. Easy for him to say. Dan was always nice to Poppa George.

Straight ahead at the nurses' station sat a young woman with a white, paper mask dangling off one ear. She glanced up from her clipboard. Poppa George explained their visit to the neonatal unit. She tapped her pen on the clipboard.

"Only two family members can visit a baby at one time, sir. I believe the baby's father is already inside the unit."

"No worries. I'll wait over there." Poppa George pointed to a chair in the hallway. The nurse turned to Maddy.

"Do you have any sniffles, a cold, or a rash?" she asked sternly. "No germs in the nursery."

For an anxious moment, Maddy did a quick inventory

of her body. Any coughing? Sneezing? Not lately. Should she mention her asthma? Better not. It wasn't contagious. She shook her head. The nurse led her to a sink and demonstrated how to scrub her hands and arms with disinfectant soap. Which, Maddy thought, could sure use some lavender oil to cover its antiseptic smell. Then the nurse steered her to the nursery door. Maddy took a deep breath. Through the window, she saw a large, brightly lit room filled with an enormous amount of equipment. Somewhere in there was her sister. And Dan. A band of panic squeezed her heart. But before she could back away, the nurse pushed open the door and ushered her through.

Along both sides of the very warm room, stretched two rows of large plastic boxes on metal stands. Above each one, square, white monitors displayed squiggly lines and flashed red lights. Everywhere, unseen motors whirred and soft beeps kept a steady beat.

Sitting on a chair next to the nearest plastic box, a woman in a soft blue uniform fed a tiny baby with the smallest bottle Maddy had ever seen. She glanced at Maddy and, with a sideways nod, pointed to the middle of the room where a man leaned over one of the plastic boxes.

Maddy clenched her hands and walked slowly towards Dan, her heart beating almost in rhythm with the beeps from the machines. She stopped a few steps behind him and stared at the two pencil-thin legs and tiny bare feet that lay very still on a white mattress inside the plastic box. Was that a baby? Was it alive? She felt light-headed, her forehead, clammy.

"Dan?" her voice wavered.

His head swiveled around.

"Maddy!" She swayed and he reached to steady her.

"You look pale," he said as he steered her to a chair behind him. "Put your head between your knees."

Maddy closed her eyes and bent down. After a minute or two, the dizziness stopped and she straightened up. In front of her, she saw a tiny baby. Her head was covered with a white cap, her bottom with a very small diaper. Wires were taped to her chest and a long, fat tube covered her nose and looped behind her head. Below her wrinkled forehead, her eyes were scrunched shut.

"What's wrong with her?" Maddy blurted.

At first, Dan didn't answer. He reached into one of the large portholes that lined the side of the box and lightly stroked the baby's arm. Then he turned towards Maddy.

"Your sister was born too early. Before her lungs were fully developed. So she needs to stay in this incubator while they mature. See that tube by her nose? It's helping her breath until she can do it all by herself."

Dan motioned Maddy to stand next to the incubator. She rose and took a small step towards it. As she watched her sister's chest quiver with each breath, her own chest tightened. She felt dizzy again and closed her eyes. Would her sister need puffers too? Or a breathing machine, like Maddy had had when she was younger?

"Put your hand in, Maddy, and touch her. She won't break."

Slowly, Maddy stretched her arm into the incubator and brushed her sister's hand. Her fingers opened and grasped Maddy's thumb.

A warm, zingy feeling ran up her arm and began to loosen the tightness inside her. Then her sister's

162

legs twitched, and the baby turned her head towards Maddy.

Wondering if her sister sensed her presence, Maddy leaned her forehead on the incubator. She watched the faint rise and fall of the baby's chest. For a few moments, they breathed together. Then, one after another, her sister's eyes opened. They were oval and gray and deep as wells. They stared at Maddy from an unknown, faraway space.

Maddy's heart swelled. She was positive her sister knew her.

"Hi, little one," Maddy whispered. "I'm Maddy, your big sister."

A hand rested on Maddy's shoulder. For a few minutes, they stood close together, she and Dan, gazing at the tiny, wizened baby who had incredibly entered their lives. In her pointy knit cap, she looked like an elf to Maddy—a very tiny one. That made Maddy smile.

"What's her name?"

"We haven't named her yet," Dan answered. "Everything happened so fast."

Without a sound, the baby let go of Maddy's finger. Her arms and legs began to pinwheel in short, jerky movements. Her skin turned a mottled red. Then the monitor started to beep in a piercing, staccato rhythm. Both Dan and Maddy jumped back as the nurse rushed towards them. She quickly checked the monitor and gauges. With sure, efficient fingers, she adjusted the wires on the baby's chest. Slowly the little arms and legs stopped wheeling. With eyes squeezed shut, the baby seemed to instantly drop into sleep.

"What was that about?" Dan frowned, rubbing the back of his neck.

"Perhaps a wire jiggled loose when she started to whirl," the nurse said, unperturbed. "Her nervous system isn't fully developed, so she's not able to handle touch very well. Best let her sleep now."

Dan instantly agreed and gave Maddy a curt sideways nod towards the door. Head bent down, Maddy followed him out of the nursery. In the hallway, Poppa George gave Dan a hug.

"How's the little one, son?"

"She's got a long way to go." Dan's shoulders sagged.

Poppa George patted his son-in-law on the back. No one said a word in the elevator as they descended to the third floor. Maddy glanced at Dan's face. It had a closed look and a familiar frown, plus dark circles under his eyes that were almost purple. He was tired, Maddy realized, but she bet he was upset with her again. He probably thought she'd squeezed her sister's hand too hard and bumped one of the wires loose.

Outside her mother's room, Dan put his finger to his lips and motioned for them to wait in the hallway. A moment later, he stepped out, said that Carla was still sleeping, and suggested they grab a late lunch in the cafeteria. Poppa George checked his watch and said they should head home before rush hour traffic. Maddy said nothing. When Dan muttered a quick goodbye without looking at her, she wished she had worn her hoodie so she could shrink inside it like a turtle. For sure Dan hadn't forgiven her for all the trouble she'd caused.

After Dan promised to stay in touch, Maddy and Poppa George made their way to the parking lot and began the long journey home. As they left the city, Maddy stared out the window, watching cars empty off ramps and shopping malls turn into fields before the highway shrunk down to two lanes. All the scenery was a shadowy backdrop to the image of her sister lying alone in an incubator miles away. What could she do? Nothing, really. Even helping her mother seemed impossible. She was so far away. And, besides, she was convinced Dan didn't want her help.

"How's Amy?" Poppa George asked out of the blue.

"Who?"

"Amy. Your friend. Didn't she go up north for the summer?"

"Uh, yeah."

"No letters?"

"Nobody writes letters, Poppa."

"Emails?"

"Dan barely ever lets me use the computer," she muttered.

It seemed ages since Maddy had thought of Amy. Her postcard. The lake. The boys on the beach. Was now a good time to visit her? Like her mother suggested not long ago? Maybe Poppa George would drive her to the cottage. She'd have to think about it. Figure out a plan. Maybe ask him at supper.

When the car pulled into the driveway, late afternoon shadows stretched over the lawn where the barn had once stood. Poppa George slid from behind the steering wheel.

"I'll heat up leftovers," he said. "Come set the table."

Instead, Maddy crossed to the fence by the grass and leaned on its top rail. A breeze rose from the creek. She thought she heard the soft clucking of hens and a faint shuffle of horses' hooves on a wooden floor. In the shadows of the cedar trees by the road, the image of a red barn wavered in the dimness. Then a furry body brushed her leg. When Maddy looked down, she saw a black cat limp away from her towards the house. Its white-tipped tail seemed to drag on the ground. Was that Shadow? Maddy watched it disappear into the woodshed. After a moment's hesitation, without a thought about supper, she ran to follow it.

Chapter 26

Inside the woodshed, the cat was nowhere to be seen. Maddy scrambled up the ladder and pushed open the small door into the attic. She glanced quickly around the room, and when she did not see the cat, she shrugged and hurried down the narrow stairs to the creamery below. Without pausing, she burst into the kitchen. In the corner, Aunt Ella rose from her rocking chair, clutching a quilt in one hand and a needle in the other. Small pieces of fabric floated to the floor around her.

"Shh, you'll wake her with your thumping!"

"Wake who?"

"The little one." Aunt Ella waved her hand at the large cookstove.

Maddy heard a small whimper. It was coming from a metal box attached to the side of the stove. She peered inside. A yellow, flannel blanket covered all but the head of a baby lying on its side. Next to it poked up a little rag doll with yellow braids and a sweet look on its face. Maddy watched the baby's mouth open and close and then open again. A long, spasmodic cough began to rack its body.

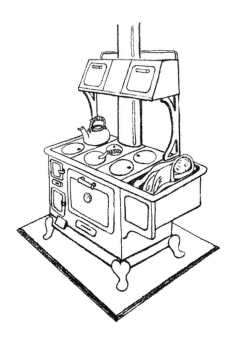

Maddy's eyes widened. "She can't breathe!"

Aunt Ella shuffled to the stove and firmly patted the baby's back until the coughing subsided into hiccups.

"Breathing's hard for the wee thing. She's only a few months old and caught the whooping cough. It's settled into her lungs. Wheezing night and day."

As Maddy stared at the wriggling, yellow bundle, a drop of saliva rolled out of the baby's mouth and its red face relaxed into sleep.

"Why is she sleeping in the stove?"

Aunt Ella settled back into the rocking chair and

gathered the quilt on her lap. Its pieces looked familiar.

"The doctor said there wasn't much to be done for her, but keeping her warm and fed. So we put her in the stove's warming tank. 'Tis the warmest place in the house and the steam from the kettle helps her breathe."

In her mind, Maddy saw the fat tube attached to her sister's nose and mouth. The wires attached to her chest. The monitor beeping away. She wasn't sure what was weirder—a baby in a stove or one in an incubator.

"There's not much that can be done for whooping cough." Aunt Ella continued. "We says our prayers. Ask the good Lord to spare her."

"Who is she?"

"Little Cora. Helen's baby."

"Aunt Helen's baby?"

Maddy was stunned. How could that be? No one had mentioned a thing about Aunt Helen being pregnant.

"Some time has passed since we've last seen you, Maddy Rose. Much has happened." Aunt Ella pointed to the teapot on the table. "Best sit yourself down, girl, and enjoy a cup of tea while I stitch this rooster onto the quilt."

Maddy felt too wound up to sit down. She stared at Baby Cora and then at the old woman bent over the quilt, her fingers trembling as she pushed the needle through the cloth.

"Lots happened in my life too," Maddy finally blurted. "Except it all happened yesterday. And today. Not, like, over a year or two."

"Aye, time has a strange way of speeding up and slowing down."

Maddy nodded but said nothing. Then the story of her sister's birth tumbled out of her. How tiny she was. How she couldn't breathe on her own. How frail and unhappy her mother seemed in the hospital. Aunt Ella listened and tried to reassure her.

"Your mother's in good hands, my dear. She'll gain her strength soon enough."

"But I wasn't there when she needed me! Even when she looked so tired. Even when I promised to stay. And then the baby came early."

"Babies come when they come, Maddy. Have faith she'll win her battle. Soon your mother will bring her home and every day she'll grow stronger, like our little Cora."

Maddy glanced again at the baby in the stove. She was sleeping peacefully. For a moment, Maddy watched the faint rise and fall of her chest.

"Dan thinks it's my fault what happened. He's pretty upset with me."

Aunt Ella looked up from her sewing. "My dear, your Dan and Helen's husband, Ray, are like loaves of bread. Crusty on the outside but possessing a softness on the inside for the wee ones. Little Cora always brings a smile to Ray's face. Be patient. Your sister will smooth her father's rough edges. And then he'll be gentler with you as well."

Maybe, Maddy thought. But she wasn't going to hold her breath.

"Aunt Ella, do you think it's true what Poppa George said about this house? That it was built in the shape of an octagon so bad air and germs couldn't stick around?"

The old woman shifted the quilt on her lap and placed a horse in position.

"That's what my father believed." She paused before adding, "It's been a good house for our family, and it'll be a good one for your family too."

Maddy felt doubtful. Whatever healing powers the octagon possessed, they hadn't worked for Eva. But then again, Eva hadn't really lived here, had she? She only visited now and then, mostly in the summers. Still, Maddy mused, it was hard to believe that the shape of a building could make a difference.

Restless, she stepped to the window and pushed its curtain aside, twisting her neck to peer across the lawn. She thought she saw a tall, slim figure striding up the road towards the house and then out of sight. A quiver of hope rose inside her.

"Aunt Ella," she asked, shifting from one foot to the other. "Is that Clare?"

"Aye, child," the woman nodded, "but he won't be here for long. Best you—"

Maddy didn't wait for another word. She darted out the side door and down the dirt driveway. Across the road, Clare was whistling for the horse munching grass in the pasture north of the mill. When it ambled close to him, he reached over the rail fence to pat its nose. As Maddy walked towards Clare, she sensed something different about him. He was taller. Leaner. Older. When the horse nudged his arm, his laugh was deeper. "Bye, ole girl, I'll miss you," he said as the horse nibbled the sugar cube in his palm. Just then, it caught sight of Maddy and shied back a step. Clare turned and stared at Maddy, his face registering neither welcome nor dismay.

Maddy flushed. She was so glad to see him but too nervous to even say hello.

Clare leaned against the fence post and crossed his arms.

"Well, Maddy. Here you are again. Turning up at the oddest times. If I close my eyes, will you disappear once again?"

Maddy's blush deepened. "I didn't mean to run away that morning," she stammered. "But all I could think of was that my Poppa George might be trying to find me . . . that something awful had happened to my mom. Which it had, so I'm glad I left when I did."

Clare straightened. "What happened, Maddy?" he asked, his eyes somber with concern.

"Well, I think Mom's going to be okay, but . . ." For a second time that morning, Maddy recounted her sister's early birth, omitting details she had told Aunt Ella but didn't know how to describe to Clare. She didn't mention Dan's name either because her feelings about him and their time together in the NICU were still as confusing as ever.

Clare listened quietly to her story and when she paused, he simply nodded and said he hoped her sister got well soon, like Baby Cora. "She gave us quite a scare," he added, "but she seems past the worst of it."

"Yeah, Aunt Ella told me not to worry about my sister, but it's hard. . . ." Maddy's words trailed away, and after a moment, her longing to know something, anything about Clare's life overwhelmed her. She took a deep breath and confessed to him about Shadow's unexpected reappearance and her hasty return to his life despite her intention to remain in her own world and deal with her own problems. "I can't help it, Clare. If that little door to the attic is open, well, I have to go through it! It's like reading a book or watching a movie, I have to know what happens next."

At first, Clare looked puzzled, but then a small grin twitched at the corners of his mouth. "No matter, Maddy. I

172

can never make sense of your comings and goings, but last time you disappeared, you left me in quite a jam. What was I supposed to do with all that fancy soap?"

"Do?" Maddy replied, a note of indignation creeping into her voice. "Sell it! That was the plan. We had it all packed and ready to go!"

"Well," said Clare, a teasing smile lighting his eyes. "That's exactly what I did. Took the whole bunch to Mrs. Franklin at the Colebrook General Store."

"Did she sell it?"

"Just about every last one."

"That's great! Did you buy an angel for Eva?"

"Not yet. They're expensive."

"That's right!" Maddy exclaimed. "I was supposed to find my two-dollar bill, and I totally forgot."

Clare swiped at the long grass by the fence, pulled up a handful, and twisted it in his hand.

"I don't need your money, Maddy," he said in a low voice. "Mother thinks I'm a good salesman and that I'll earn a good wage workin' in Toronto."

"Toronto? You're moving to Toronto?"

Clare ducked his head away from the disbelief etched on Maddy's face. With a toss of his wrist, he threw the ball of grass towards the horse and watched it munch his offering. Then he turned to Maddy and held up his hands.

"I'm sorry, Maddy, but I have to go. After Eva died, Mother packed up her belongings and moved to Toronto, just like I mentioned a while back. She wanted me to join her right away, but Aunt Ella convinced her to let me finish my schoolin' here. Now that I've got a diploma, it's time to find a job and the city has lots to offer."

Maddy, kicked at a rock in the dirt road and sent it skittering into the weeds. It was just as she feared. Clare was moving to Toronto, and she would never see him again. It seemed like he had changed into a young man overnight, even though she knew two years had passed in his time, two whole years in which she hadn't a chance to connect with him. Did he care those months had passed without spending a minute with her? Did he care that they might never see each other again? The likely answer pierced her heart. Obviously, he had already made plans that couldn't possibly include her. His life had moved on, and now she realized, with a growing despondency, she had to do the same—return to her own time and her own family. And never see him again.

Maddy felt Clare's eyes on her, searching for the reason she was so quiet. But her throat tightened and stifled the questions her heart wanted to ask, the ones she feared couldn't be answered to her liking. She turned away from Clare and propped her elbows on the fence's top rail, staring into the distance which seemed to stretch forever.

As if sensing her confusion, Clare, too, leaned on the rail, but an arm's length away. Just then, a dragonfly darted out of the reeds by the mill pond and hovered in front of them. Clare held out his arm and it landed on his sleeve for a second before flying away.

As they watched it zip back and forth above the water, Clare's face wore a familiar faraway look. He said softly, "Eva loved dragonflies. Each summer she wished she could be a dragonfly for a day, 'cause they're always flying in the sunshine. Said she wanted to soar over the fields and see the world from a diff'rent perspective. You know she really did have a dragonfly spirit. She never stopped moving. Until she got sick. Even then, she'd sit outside on a blanket when the days were warm. Them little red ones would land on her arms. Her face too."

When the dragonfly disappeared out of sight, he turned towards Maddy. His eyes were soft with sadness. Full of her own bewildering feelings, Maddy simply said, "I'm sorry, Clare," and then added, "for everything."

As if understanding exactly what she meant, Clare nodded his head once, straightened, and glanced across the road to the house. "Uncle Ray'll be here soon to take me to the train. It's time to hitch up the wagon."

He opened the pasture gate and caught the horse by its halter. Without another word, he led the horse to the barn. Maddy followed a few steps behind. With increasing numbness, she watched him harness the horse, slide the bridle over its head, and attach the straps to the wagon. Behind its seats, she spotted a trunk and suitcase, packed and ready to go. She crossed her arms and squeezed them tightly against her body, willing herself not to cry. This was it, their goodbye. But she had no idea what to say. *Bye, see you again, come back soon, I'll miss you*—all sounded hopelessly inadequate to express the loss that threatened to overwhelm her.

Voices in the driveway drifted into the barn as Uncle Ray and Aunt Helen called to Aunt Ella. Clare patted the horse's rump, adjusted its halter, and finally turned towards Maddy.

"We'll be off now. Don't want to miss the train."

Maddy barely managed a nod. She longed to hug him, but she felt too awkward and shy. Instead she thrust out her hand. Clare stared at it and then grinned. He reached past it for her shoulders and gave her a quick, firm hug. Then he tugged on his cap, picked up the horse's reins, and led it out of the barn. Maddy dodged away from the wagon's rolling wheels and hid in the shadow of the barn door.

"Bye," she whispered. Whether he heard her or not above his family's greetings, she couldn't tell. Tears blurred her eyes as she watched his aunt and uncle mount the wagon's step and settle on its seats. Before Clare climbed up, Aunt Ella wrapped her arms around him for a long, parting hug. When she let go, she patted his arm and slipped a small package into his hand. Finally, the wagon rolled along the driveway and onto the road. Maddy darted out of the barn. Just as Clare disappeared down the road, she lifted her arms and waved a slow, final goodbye with her whole heart.

From the doorway, Aunt Ella beckoned Maddy into the kitchen.

"He'll be back, my dear," she said as she patted Maddy's arm. "He's a country lad at heart and sure to return for visits." Then she shuffled towards the creamery. "Did Clare mention that he left something for you?"

With a shaky finger she pointed to a bundle on the shelf above the sink. It was small, dusty package wrapped in brown paper and tied with string. As Maddy reached for it, a baby's cry erupted from the kitchen.

"The wee one. She's needing my attention," Aunt Ella said. "Best take the bundle upstairs."

Maddy hesitated. She didn't want to leave. But Aunt Ella patted her back with brisk reassurance. "'Tis a good family you live with, Maddy. Take heart."

Maddy returned her hug. The old woman's shoulders felt thin underneath her shawl. "Bye," she whispered as

Aunt Ella shuffled to the kitchen to calm Cora's loud cries. Maddy slowly dragged herself up the stairs to the attic. On the bed, the black cat blinked its yellow eyes at her. As Maddy sank beside it, dust rose from the mattress and tickled her nose. She rubbed it hard trying to quell the urge to sneeze. Through the tears that rose in her eyes, she looked around the room and wondered if she would ever see its jumble of furniture again. Some things were already missing.

Where was the wicker doll carriage? The wooden rocking horse? Had they been rescued for Baby Cora? And where were Eva's dress and hat? They no longer hung from the hook on the wall. She wasn't sure, but now that she thought about it, bits of Aunt Ella's quilt looked like Eva's dress. And yes! exactly like parts of the quilt folded into the trunk in her loft.

Maddy brushed the dust off the package on her lap. She untied the string's simple knot and folded back the brown paper to reveal the words *Sander Soap* printed on a worn, narrow cardboard box. Inside it, she discovered a single sheet of paper folded on top of two dented bars of soap. Maddy opened it and read—

Maddy, you were right. All the soap sold. Except these bars that fell off the counter. Missus Franklin told me to give them to my mother, but I thought you might want them. Poor Shadow's gone lame and don't climb to the attic anymore. Maybe that's why you haven't visited us in some time, but since I never seen that small door you claim is up there, I'm not sure the reason for you staying away. But no matter, just know that I'm obliged for your ideas and I reckon you'll find a splendid way to settle your family troubles. Clare

As Maddy read Clare's note, a warm tingle spread

through her body. Did he really appreciate her ideas? Did he really have faith she could solve her own problems? But why, then, hadn't he said so while they stood by the fence or when he hugged her goodbye? She read the note again. An inner glow began to replace the tension inside her. She remembered how shy Clare could be, that he seldom expressed his emotions, except for that awful time in the barn. But she deserved his anger then, so it felt wonderful to realize that he had truly forgiven her and that he actually believed in her.

Maddy reached into the box and picked up one of lavender soaps. She held it to her nose and closed her eyes. Its heady, floral scent brought back happy memories of making soap together. Shaving the large block and melting it on the stove. Stirring and stirring while it bubbled. Even the ache in her shoulders and the pain of hot splatter on her hand. Especially the lavender oil rubbed on their cuts and burns. At that moment, Maddy understood that maybe it hadn't been a bad thing to push Clare into their soap project. In an unanticipated way, it had worked out. Certainly not the way she had fervently hoped, but with a resolution she could live with. Life seemed to be like that. You could make plans, some of the best, but when they fell apart . . . well, they fell apart. But maybe something good could be gathered from the pieces.

"You know," Maddy said to Shadow who slowly raised her head when she heard Maddy's voice. "Clare will make a great salesman 'cause he's such a hard worker. And he doesn't fool around once he sets his mind to something."

As if she agreed, the cat began to purr. Maddy reached over to stroke its fur. It felt thin and coarse.

"You're old, aren't you, kitty," she whispered. "I saw you limp into the woodshed. Clare said you don't climb up here anymore, but you found me today and then made it back up the ladder." Shadow twitched her white-tipped tail and tucked herself into a tight ball. She closed her eyes but continued to purr. Maddy wondered how old she was. She understood then that the cat, too, might never see Clare again.

Everything from the past was slipping away. Eva. Clare. Aunt Ella. Even Shadow.

For a moment, Maddy sat very still on the bed. In the expanding quietness of the attic, noises from the kitchen below rose through the grate—the rocking chair squeaking on the kitchen's wooden floor, Aunt Ella's soft crooning, the baby's cries fading to hiccups and then silence. A gentle voice inside Maddy, much like Aunt Ella's, whispered, *Life goes on here, Maddy. And in your time too. Go and seek it.*

On the attic wall, the outline of the small door to the woodshed wavered. Maddy slipped Clare's letter in the soap box and closed its lid. With a gentle pat on Shadow's head, she crossed the floor and pushed her way back into her own time. Behind her, the door faded away.

Chapter 27

M addy had little patience for the rain that kept her indoors for the next two whole days. Especially when it poured buckets. On the second day, she woke to a crack of thunder, followed by a windy cloudburst that rattled her bedroom window. In the kitchen, so much water streamed down the windows, she could barely see the mud puddles drowning her mother's garden.

"Mom, won't like that," she said with alarm when she spotted the zinnias, their heads bowed to the ground.

Poppa George looked up from his newspaper.

"Like what?"

"The garden's a huge mess."

"Not to worry," Poppa George said as he turned a page. "A day of sunshine will fix things up."

Maddy didn't agree. It would take more than a day of sunshine to straighten those battered plants. All the rain was making her depressed.

She wished the internet was working. Or that she had a movie to watch. Something to replace the jumble of scenes that had been reeling through her head since she woke up. They were like two movies playing on the same screen at the same time—one, a scene of Clare climbing into the wagon, and the other, a scene of her sister lying in the incubator at the hospital. She wasn't resigned to the ending of the first one. And she worried all the time about how the second one would play out. She felt like she should just go back to bed and pull the blanket over her head.

But when she retreated to her bedroom, she tripped over the box of soaps she had left on the floor next to her nightstand.

"Oh, no. . . ." She groaned as the smell of lavender tickled her nose. One by one, she carefully removed them from the box and smoothed their wrappers. Then she knelt down and pulled her Private Box from under the bed.

Inside it lay the empty case for her missing Dominion of Canada two-dollar bill. Where was it? She glanced around her room and spotted her backpack in the corner where she had flung it that awful night not so long ago. With a sigh, she rescued it and opened its flap. When she rummaged inside for the bill, her fingers brushed against a crumpled paper. The lavender soap recipe. She unfolded it slowly and reread its instructions and, at the bottom, its claim to heal and calm those who used it. Maddy sat back on her heels and smiled. Another idea was taking shape in her head.

She rushed down the stairs to the living room. Under a pile of magazines on the coffee table, she dug out her mother's book on soapmaking. There on page sixty-seven, she found a recipe for babies with sensitive skin. It used plain, white soap bars like the ones her mother had stored in the bathroom cupboard. Maddy's eyes skimmed the list of ingredients.

There was lavender oil! How lucky was that? She was sure there was enough left for this new recipe. And coconut and olive oil. Plenty of that in the kitchen cupboard. But jojoba oil? She'd never heard of it. The book said it contained vitamin E for soothing baby skin. Hmm, maybe the drug store carried it. She'd ride there as soon as the rain stopped. What a great idea! She couldn't wait to start making this special baby soap.

But the rain poured down all day. By lunchtime, Maddy's impatience had turned into resignation. With a long-suffering sigh, she realized that she'd have to wait until tomorrow to pedal into town. So when Poppa George closed his eyes for his daily snooze, she buzzed around and gathered up all the other ingredients. Soap bars and lavender oil from the bathroom cupboard. Coconut and olive oil from the kitchen cupboard. And distilled water from the shelf above the washing machine. All these things she stashed in a box in the corner of the creamery.

Then she checked the kitchen shelves for utensils. Glass bowls. Measuring cup. Grater. Double boiler. Mixing spoons. What about a mold for the soap? The recipe suggested a muffin tin rubbed with oil. That was easy. There was one in the drawer under the stove. She was ready to go. All she needed was the jojoba oil and a block of time when no one was home to make this fabulous soap. She couldn't think of a better baby present to give her mom.

By early evening, the rain had slowed to a drizzle. After supper, it had ceased altogether, and a watery moon shone through the last of the storm clouds racing away to the east.

*****

In the morning, as Maddy rinsed her cereal bowl in the sink, Poppa George put down his coffee cup and announced that the bookstore two towns over had rung to say his book order had arrived.

"I think I'll drive there later this morning and pick it up. Will you be all right by yourself for a few hours?"

"Sure, Poppa. No problem." Maddy could barely contain her delight at this news. She'd have just enough time to make the healing baby soap.

"I'm going for a bike ride," she said. "Before it gets hot." After a peck on her grandfather's cheek and a quick goodbye, she wheeled her bike out of the garage. The cool, morning air felt fresh on her face as she skirted the puddles. In town, the drug store had just opened. The clerk, all smiles, helped Maddy find a small bottle of jojoba oil in the cosmetics section.

"It's made from the seeds of a desert bush. A great moisturizer for your whole body," she said as she handed it to Maddy. "But it's expensive!"

Maddy gulped when she saw the price. She wouldn't have enough money left for more wrapping paper. But the bottle label claimed it was the perfect oil for sensitive skin. So Maddy paid for it, tucked it into her backpack, and headed home.

"Maddy! Thank goodness you're back!" Poppa George greeted her when she wheeled into the driveway. "I'm on my way to the bookstore now. I left you a sandwich on the counter."

He opened his car door and climbed into the driver's seat.

"And there's good news," he said, rolling down the window. "Dan called. He said Carla finally held your sister this morning and fed her!"

"That's great!" Maddy exclaimed. "But are they coming home today?" Maddy held her breath. Would she have time to make her soap?

Poppa George shook his head. "'Fraid not, hon. She's still a little tyke with a long way to go. When your mother's feeling better, they'll find a place to stay near the hospital for a few weeks."

Maddy exhaled. "When can we visit them?"

"Perhaps in a day or two. Carla needs clean clothes. Dan asked if you could pack some for her. Think you can manage that?

"No problem."

With a wave, Poppa George backed his car out of the driveway.

Once inside the house, Maddy dashed upstairs, selected a clean nightie, underwear, and three summer dresses for her mother, and folded them into a tote bag. Then she rushed downstairs and, after propping the soap recipe book on the kitchen table, carefully reread the directions. It was important to have all the ingredients ready beforehand. She wished Clare was here to help her. They had worked hard together in the factory making their lavender soap. Could she do it without him?

First step was to grate the soap. Last time, she had scraped her knuckles. Now she'd be more careful. One at a time, she rubbed the white bars up and down the sharp grater. It was still hard work! Her fingers ached. But eventually, the bars turned into a pile of shavings on the kitchen table. And on the floor. She'd sweep those up later. After she scooped the ones off the table into the top pan of the double boiler, she added the water. Then she poured in the olive and coconut oils and mixed them all together. When the water in the bottom pan started to boil, she turned it down to a simmer. Now came the long, hard part of stirring and watching the soap melt. She remembered not to let it bubble. Just melt.

As Maddy stirred and stirred, her stomach started to rumble. She eyed the cheese sandwich on the counter. No harm eating it while she worked. But when she bit into it, a chunk of bread fell into the pan. Shocked, Maddy stared at it sinking into the soap. Afraid it would wreck the recipe, she dropped her sandwich on the stove, spooned the chunk out of the pot, and dumped it in the sink, where it floated like a miniature iceberg around the dirty dishes.

After that scare, Maddy paid careful attention to her stirring. The soap slowly melted. Eventually it looked like cottage cheese and then it turned stringy. Finally, it thickened. With two hands, she carried the hot pot to the counter and carefully rested it on the wooden cutting board. Now was the time to add the jojoba and lavender oils. The soap smelled wonderful, but Maddy thought it looked boringly plain. The recipe suggested colorants. What were they? Then she remembered that Grammy Bea used to drop food coloring into her cake icing.

Maddy swung open the cupboard door and plucked the box of little plastic bottles off the shelf. She squirted all the red and a lot of the blue into the soap. Then she stirred and stirred until it turned a light lavender, just like the lilacs in her grandmother's garden. Maddy smiled. It looked good enough to eat. But it was starting to harden. With a soup ladle, she quickly scooped it into the muffin tin, spilling large drops over the counter. No matter, she'd clean it all up later.

At last, Maddy stepped back and surveyed the tin brimming with twelve cupcake-shaped soaps. Should she stick a tiny chimney in one so that it looked like the octagon? She quickly cut a rectangle from a piece of red construction paper, taped it onto a toothpick, and poked it in the middle soap. After they hardened, she'd find Grammy Bea's Christmas canister, fill it with the pretty soaps, and tape a big purple bow on its lid. Her mother was going to love this baby gift, and maybe Dan would laugh at her joke.

With a contented but exhausted sigh, Maddy plopped onto the sofa in the kitchen corner. Within minutes, she was fast asleep.

The thud of heavy footsteps woke her as the kitchen door swung open with a whoosh.

"Madison Rose Stevens! What's going on here?"

Dan stood only a few feet away, his mouth gaping, his eyes widened in furious disbelief.

Chapter 28

Maddy sat bolt upright on the sofa and blinked. Her eyes followed Dan's angry gaze around the kitchen. They saw the soap shavings scattered on the floor, the dirty dishes piled high in the sink, the counter covered with soap spills and empty bottles. When her eyes stopped on the frown darkening Dan's face, she began to feel scared, like a trapped animal. He turned towards her.

"First thing, Maddy," he said, his eyes narrowing, "when I came home, I almost ran over your bike in the driveway. Now, this mess in the kitchen. I repeat, what's going on here?"

Maddy rose shakily to her feet. "I'm making something."

"I'll say! You're making a mess! A huge mess!"

Dan stepped towards the counter and waved his hand at the muffin tin.

"What's all this stuff?"

"Don't touch!"

"Did you get into Carla's soap supplies?"

Maddy did not answer.

"I thought I made it very clear that there were to be no soap projects started in this kitchen before, or even after, the baby arrived. What possessed you to try such a stunt?"

Maddy looked at the lavender orbs in the muffin tin. Couldn't he see how pretty they were? Why did he only see the mess? Tears filled her eyes. She bent her head so he couldn't see them.

"Listen, young lady. You'll have to do better than this. You need to stop thinking of just yourself and start paying attention to what your mother needs so she can look after your sister without worrying about you."

Maddy's head jerked up. That was way too unfair. She felt the tips of her ears redden. A buzz like angry bees rose in her head. She raised her chin. "That's soap for babies with sensitive skin. I made it especially for my sister."

Then as she retreated towards the kitchen door, before she lost her nerve, she took a big breath and exhaled her words in a rush. "Why are you always mad at me? Why do you never ever like what I do, even when I'm trying hard to help?"

Before he could see her tears, Maddy ran out the kitchen door, hopped on her bike, and raced down the road.

By the time she turned the corner onto the county road towards town, her tears had dried, but her heart raced with the injustice of it all. Dan was never going to understand her. Or be nice to her. She was sure she couldn't live with him anymore. It was high time to find her own father and beg him to take her in, even if he lived on the other side of the world.

Maddy pedled furiously, writing and rewriting in her head the letter she would send to her father if only she could discover his address. By the time she reached Victoria Park, another idea had surfaced in her mind. She wheeled her bike to the stand in front of the town hall building. She would email Amy from the library . . . much simpler, much faster than locating her father. Then she'd escape north to Amy's cottage as soon as possible. If Poppa George wouldn't drive her, she'd take the bus.

Fifteen minutes later, after she had tapped the send button on a long email, Maddy plopped down on the hot cement steps outside the building to wait for Amy's reply. She wished she had shoved some change in her pocket before she left. Then she could buy a pop and something to eat. She didn't know what else to do while she waited.

Across the road, the empty bench in front of the water fountain beckoned her to stretch out in the shade. The last time she had done that, she had met Janine and her little brother. She remembered they had invited her to visit them. If her plans to escape to Amy's cottage didn't work out, she could make friends with them and hang out at their house. Anything was better than staying home all the time. Maybe now was a good time to find out where they lived. Near the school, Janine had told her. And there was something about a boat in the driveway.

Maddy pulled her bike out of the stand and slowly pedaled along the main road, peering up every crossroad until she saw the school a block to the south. Next door to it, *The Merry Mermaid* perched high and dry next to a row of pine trees. But there were no cars parked in the driveway and the house looked dark and locked up.

No one was home. Well, that was another good idea down the drain. She turned her bike around and pedaled to the library to check if Amy had emailed her back. But when she glided to a stop in front of the town hall, she saw that the library had closed early for the day. Tired and discouraged, Maddy decided to go home. She hoped that, by now, Dan had found the clothes she had packed for her mother and left.

Slowing down a block before her street, she spotted a small street sign perched on top of a rusty pole. Its red letters flickered through the branches of a cedar tree—*East Colebrook Cemetery*. An arrow pointed south. Maddy jammed on her brakes and gazed at the side road that disappeared down the hill. Could that be the cemetery were Eva had been buried?

Maddy slowly coasted towards the lake. Just over a rise, a narrow graveyard stretched along the road. She leaned her bike against its iron fence, slipped the chain off the gate, and squeezed through. On one side of a gravel drive, rows of shiny, new gravestones, with flowerpots propped next to them, filled the cemetery.

On the other side, old, gray stones leaned at odd angles in the grass. Maddy wandered around them, squinting at names chiseled on their surfaces. Many were worn away by weather or were covered by peeling, brown lichen. Was Eva's grave here? Could she find it? She didn't even know Eva's last name.

Close to an old oak tree with gnarled branches, a chunky, squared stone stood by itself. Grass grew close to its base. There were no flowers. But on its surface, a carved angel spread its wings along the top of the gravestone.

Maddy slowly approached it and crouched down, squinting at its shallow, script letters.

Eva Foster

1889–1901

An odd tingle crept up Maddy's spine. Here, lying beneath her feet, was Clare's sister. How strange to finally be this close to her, and yet be so separated by grass, dirt, and a hundred years. Kneeling on the damp ground, she traced the winged figure, its round face framed by curls of hair, its tender smile, its feather wingtips circling the words carved below. It was the perfect angel to watch over Eva. Maddy was proud that she and Clare had made such great soap and that he'd sold it and then earned more money to buy the best angel.

Beams of sunlight shone through the leaves of the oak tree and bathed the angel and Maddy in a soft light. She sat back and, for a few minutes, pulled up blades of grass and let them fall between her fingers. Her thoughts drifted to the girl she had glimpsed in the old kitchen, the lively spirit who rescued baby chicks and dreamed of flying like dragonflies. She wished that she had spent a day with her, just hanging around in the barn and perhaps playing with Shadow's kittens, for surely a litter would have been born that summer in the loft among the hay bales.

When a warm breeze blew over Maddy's face, she closed her eyes and listened to the seagulls circling overhead. Then faint laughter, like the tinkle of distant chimes, filled the air. Her eyes flickered open and rested on the angel.

Eva Foster
1889 ~ 1901

A brilliant green dragonfly had settled on Eva's gravestone, its lacy wings sparkling in the sunshine. Like a tiny arrow, it shot upwards past Maddy's head and swooped back, zigzagging in figure eights, over and over again, until it stopped inches from her face.

Mesmerized, Maddy watched the delicate creature hovering in the air. Then it zipped to the angel on the gravestone and back again, landing on Maddy's forearm, where it gazed at her with its large, green eyes. Maddy held her breath, lost in its stare. With giddy delight, she sensed that the dragonfly was Eva's spirit. Ever so lightly, she felt her own spirit lift in the air. For an eternal moment it seemed as if they soared together in the golden sunshine above the oak tree.

Then the emerald dragonfly swooped past Eva's gravestone and with a flash of its gossamer wings, darted away towards the wide lake. Maddy watched it fly to the horizon and disappear where the blue of the water met the blue of the sky.

A sense of calm floated down on Maddy. For the first time in weeks, she felt untroubled, even happy. She felt that Eva had given her a gift, a message of reassurance that all was well. It echoed the gentle reminder of Aunt Ella's parting words—*'Tis a good family you live with, Maddy. Take heart.* The anger inside her began to melt away, along with the desire to escape her life. She sensed that taking heart meant having courage to face the challenges in her life, and also having faith that somehow most things would work out well for her. She might lose heart sometimes, and then life might get hard again, but she felt more confident that she could now cope with such changes.

With the blue sky overhead and the shining lake in the distance, the cemetery had become a peaceful resting place. Maddy closed her eyes and relaxed into its quiet, her breath rising and falling in a deep and peaceful rhythm.

Moments later, or maybe longer, blue jays began to quarrel in the oak tree. The sun was sinking towards the horizon and stretching the shadows of the tree branches around her. It was late. Time to go home.

Chapter 29

When Maddy parked her bike in the garage, she glanced at the woodshed door, imagining the loft. Soon, but not right away, she'd pull the quilt out of the trunk. Maybe she'd give it to her mother and tell her about the woman who made it, and about the family who had lived in their house a hundred years ago. She wished she knew what had happened to Aunt Ella. That last day together, the old woman had seemed much older; her hands had trembled as she threaded the needle, her back was more stooped. And what about the baby who slept in the woodstove? Maddy smiled wistfully. Did little Cora get better? Had the octagon's healing properties saved her? Did she grow up there with sisters or brothers?

Maddy hated not knowing the end of this story. She was afraid its last chapter had been torn out and lost. Like the story of her father. She didn't know what had happened to him either, where he went, why he never came back.

Maybe, deep down, his leaving was the reason it was hard for her to trust Dan. What kind of father might Dan be? One who left? Or one who stayed, looked past her faults, and loved her?

As Maddy closed the garage door, she heard the phone ring, then Poppa George's voice. "She just came home. I'll get her right away."

Her grandfather came to the door carrying the receiver on its long cord, his hand pressed over the mouthpiece. He hurriedly motioned to Maddy to come inside.

"Your mother," he silently mouthed.

Maddy took a deep breath. "Hi, Mom," she said, walking the phone into the privacy of the living room. "Please don't worry," she began, but then listened quietly to her mother's words before promising not to disappear again.

When she returned to the kitchen and hung up, Poppa George raised an eyebrow at her, prompting Maddy to shrug. "She wants me to visit her . . . tomorrow . . . in the hospital. Can you drive me there?"

"Sure thing, Maddy. I already promised Carla I'd do that after her third call. She was so worried about you. Apparently, Dan told her the whole story about coming home and finding the kitchen in an uproar and you storming away on your bike. He went to look for you. And then, when he saw your bike at the library, he thought he'd give you time to cool off."

Maddy was taken aback. Dan had gone to look for her? Why? She was relieved he hadn't tried to drag her home.

"I'm fine, Poppa," she replied defensively. "I was at the library the whole time. I wasn't gone that long." Maddy didn't want to tell him, or anyone, about the cemetery. That was private. Maybe for always. Then she noticed the apron tied around his waist. She turned around and surveyed the kitchen. The soap shavings on the table and the floor were gone. The stove sparkled. The countertop was spotless. All the dishes in the sink had been washed and were drying in the rack.

"Did you clean up that whole mess?" she asked incredulously.

"Wasn't much to do while I waited for you between phone calls." He winked at her.

Maddy laughed. "You're a total fairy godfather!"

Poppa George held out the sides of the apron and bowed towards her.

"You sure can make a mess," he chuckled. Then, nodding at the cupcake tin, he added, "But they're real pretty. And they smell nice. Did you know there used to be a mill across the street? Complete with a waterwheel. Apparently, around the turn of the century they made soap there!"

Maddy gaped at her grandfather. "Really?" she stammered. "I ... I ... just found the soap recipe in one of Mom's books. And she had all the supplies in the bathroom cupboard and ... and ... "

Poppa George shot her a quizzical look. Maddy blushed. She glanced away, unsure of what to confess.

"They're for my sister."

He gave her one more long, wordless stare and then untied his apron. "I must say, you worked mighty hard making that soap. We'll take it to your mom tomorrow."

Maddy nodded, relieved her grandfather didn't ask any more questions.

*****

In the morning, Maddy smoothed the last of the purple ribbon she found lying on her bedroom floor. She tied it into a bow and taped it on the lid of the Christmas canister. Inside, the lavender soaps nestled in the purple tissue paper. Even the one with the chimney stuck in it. During the drive to the hospital, she cradled them carefully on her lap.

Before the traffic thickened in the city, Maddy told Poppa George that she had emailed Amy and asked if she could visit her at the cottage.

"If Amy's mother says 'yes,' will you drive me there?"

"It's quite the trip, Maddy. Let's talk to your mother before we make any plans."

That sounded promising. She grinned and thought about what she'd pack in her suitcase—bathing suit, sunglasses, sunscreen, beach towel, lots of shorts, and her new jeans. Maybe she'd buy a few tops at the mall. All she had at home were T-shirts.

Before Maddy realized it, they had reached the hospital and pulled into the car park. It wasn't until they pushed the buttons in the elevator that Maddy thought of Dan. Her stomach tightened into a familiar knot. She hoped desperately he wouldn't be in her mother's room. But when they pushed open its door, neither Dan nor her mother were there.

"Check the neonatal nursery," suggested a passing nurse. "She spends a lot of time there."

"Best leave your present here," said Poppa George. "They won't let you take it into the nursery." Maddy reluctantly set her gift on the dresser and followed her grandfather back to the elevator.

Upstairs on the seventh floor, Maddy scrubbed her

hands and arms to her elbows. In the nursery, she spotted her mother right away. She was sitting in a rocking chair next to her sister's incubator, holding a tiny bundle against her chest. Her eyes were closed as she gently rocked back and forth. Maddy watched for a moment. She thought her mother looked beautiful. Her shiny hair fell loosely over cheeks that bloomed like pink roses. A contented smile played on her lips.

"Mom?" Maddy said softly.

Her mother's eyes flew open. "Maddy! You're here!" The bundle in her arms wriggled. Maddy watched her sister's face scrunch up and relax without a sound. She looked plumper, less red and wrinkly, more like a real baby.

With one finger, Carla carefully adjusted the breathing tube taped to the baby's nose. Maddy noticed she was breathing more easily since the last time she had seen her.

"I know she looks fragile," Carla said, "but she's getting stronger every day. I can feed her my milk now, from a preemie bottle." She nodded at a small bottle perched on the stand close to her.

Maddy smiled a tiny, hesitant smile. She didn't dare reach out and touch her sister. Instead she pulled a small chair next to her mother and leaned against her shoulder.

"What's her name?" she whispered.

"Dan wants to name her after me. But I think she needs her own name." Carla gently touched the baby's nose. "Any suggestions?"

Maddy thought about the baby cradled in the stove. "What about Cora?" she asked shyly.

"Hmm, Cora seems a bit old-fashioned."

"Or Coralee?"

"That's pretty, but quite unusual. Where did you hear that name?"

Maddy shrugged. It had just popped into her head. It sounded like beads on a beautiful necklace like the pale peach one Grandma Bea used to wear.

"Mom," Maddy said as they watched the baby sleep. "I brought you a present. Something I made for my sister."

"So I heard," her mother laughed.

Maddy grinned. "Yeah, I really messed up the kitchen. But they turned out really good. They're in your room."

"Well then, let's put Coralee in her bed and check out this mysterious gift."

Carla pushed a button to summon the nurse who helped her move the baby to the incubator. Then Maddy took her mother's arm and walked with her to the wheelchair outside the nursery door where Poppa George greeted them with hugs. Down the hall the elevator door opened, and Dan stepped out carrying a small, bright green, gift bag.

"Ah, Maddy," he said, his face solemn. "Just the person I want to see." He held the bag out to her. "A peace offering . . . for being such a grump yesterday."

Maddy didn't move. Who was he calling a grump? He was the one who had yelled at her. But, then again, she had shouted back and stomped out the door. Maddy glanced at Poppa George who was examining the ceiling. She turned to her mother. She was staring straight at her husband, her head jerking slightly in Maddy's direction. Finally, Dan stepped forward.

"I guess I overdid the yelling part, Maddy. I'm sorry. I haven't had much sleep lately . . . and I've been stressed out and . . ."

"It's okay, Dan," Maddy said quietly. "I'm sorry I didn't clean things up right away, but I was really tired too and," she added, looking shyly at him, "a little stressed out myself."

Poppa George snorted. Her mother laughed out loud. And the corner of Dan's mouth twitched into a grin. Maddy reached forward and took the gift bag from his outstretched hand.

*****

Chapter 30

Two days later, all the way to Amy's cottage, Maddy held her new Nokia cell phone in one hand. With the other, she slid its cover open every few minutes to gently run her fingers over the buttons. She still couldn't believe that Dan had bought it for her.

"To call your mom," he had said when she'd opened the gift bag. "It's a great way to stay in touch." Then he gave her a quick lesson in how the phone worked.

"Until you have a job, your mom and I will pay for a basic plan. Every month, you have twenty-five free calls during the day. At night, unlimited."

Before she left home that morning to head to Amy's cottage, Dan had patted her shoulder. "Just call me, Maddy, if you have any problems. Or if you need anything."

Maddy had blinked at him. "Thanks, I will," she mumbled, surprised that he wished to stay in touch with her.

But Maddy soon discovered that she could make very

few calls while visiting Amy. There were no cell phone towers along the highway as she and Poppa George drove north, and the cottages by the lake had no reception. But the cell phone had a small camera. She and Amy took as many pictures as the memory card could hold.

Three weeks later, when she returned home, Dan downloaded them into the iMac and showed her how to send them to Amy.

"Mom," she breathed excitedly into her phone as she sat on the patio. "I can't wait to show you the pictures I took at the cottage. There's tons of me on the beach. And at the clubhouse with all Amy's friends. And at the bonfire we had the last night. It was great!"

"Absolutely marvelous." Her mother laughed. "And I can't wait to show you how much Coralee has grown. The doctor thinks we can take her home in a few days. By the way, all the nurses were impressed with the baby soap you made her. They think it's just right for her tender skin."

Maddy's heart swelled. She envisioned bathing Coralee with the special soap. Dan had bought a small baby tub that fit inside the sink. It even had pockets for holding soap and baby shampoo. Maddy wondered how the soap would feel sliding over her sister's arms and legs.

The day before her mother and Coralee's grand arrival, Maddy folded the baby towels and washcloths on the bathroom shelf and tidied the baby clothes and diapers in her mother's bedroom. In her own bedroom, she picked all her clothes off the floor and dusted the furniture. As she straightened her father's photograph on her dresser, the wish to see him surged inside of her and then subsided with a small sigh. Maybe someday she'd try to find him. Maybe her mother would even help her, but now their lives were full with caring for baby Coralee. Later that afternoon, without being asked, Maddy vacuumed the kitchen and living room floors. While pushing the hose back and forth, she realized that she hadn't used her puffer in a while. Hardly at the cottage. And not since she returned home. Had the octagon's shape pushed the tension out of the house and let its air flow easily around her? Maddy wasn't sure, but she also wasn't going to worry about it at the moment.

Finally, on the weekend, all was ready. When they came home, Dan carefully carried the tiny baby upstairs to a crib squeezed in their bedroom corner. He also tucked Carla into bed for a nap and kissed her forehead.

In the afternoon, when everyone was awake, Dan helped Carla wrap Coralee in a special shirt that held the baby close to her chest. Inside its kangaroo pouch, the little one slept peacefully right through Poppa George's special macaroni and cheese supper.

The next morning, Maddy was surprised to see Dan carrying Coralee in the kangaroo shirt while he made breakfast for everyone. Wearing an apron, he hummed as he flipped pancakes onto a platter and slid them onto the table.

Maddy reached for her cell phone and snapped a picture. Dan's eyebrows shot up and he covered his mouth in mock horror.

"No blackmail," he said with a wink.

Maddy grinned and shook her head. This was a new Dan. Dan the Dad. She suppressed a giggle at the thought. She still wasn't sure how she felt about him, but a tiny, warm glow inside, like sunshine on an early spring day, promised happier days ahead.

"Dan," she asked. "Do you have Janine's phone number?

"Janine?"

"Yeah, the girl I met before Coralee was born. You told me her father works with you."

"Right! I wrote their house number down somewhere." He fumbled for his wallet in his pocket under the apron. Pieces of paper fell out of it as he searched for the right one. Maddy slid off her chair, gathered them up, and shyly handed them back to him.

"Here," he said, giving her a small scrap. "They may not be back yet from their trip, but give it a try."

Maddy carefully tapped the number into her cell phone under Janine's name. Maybe she'd call her later that day or tomorrow. It seemed like a good time to find a friend in her own town, in her own time.

After she slipped her dishes into the dishwasher, she wandered outside and plunked down on the sun-warmed steps of the front porch. She rested her chin on her hands and peered across the street. There, on the concrete stoop of the neighbor's bungalow, a fluffy black cat licked its fur in a slow, steady rhythm. It lazily raised its head and stared at Maddy with enormous, yellow eyes. All of a sudden, it sprang up and meowed loudly, over and over, until the door swung open and the white-haired woman stepped outside.

"Did you get another mouse, kitty?"

The cat meowed once more.

The woman shaded her eyes with one hand and, following the cat's stare, squinted across the street at Maddy.

"Ah, Maddy," she called. "I noticed your grandfather left early this morning. I bet you miss him. Come join me and Shadow for a cup of tea."

An electric shock shot up through Maddy. For a moment she was unable to breath or move. Then, with the queerest of feelings, as if an invisible force was pulling her forward, she crossed the street towards the old woman, who held the door open for her. When she reached the steps, the cat flicked its fluffy tail and darted into the house. Maddy followed, her heart racing inside her.

In the kitchen, beams of sunlight seemed to float back and forth like spotlights on a stage. They illuminated the delicate pattern of pink apple blossoms on a teapot and the purple and white asters painted on the back of a rocking chair. Maddy felt dizzy. She reached for the doorframe to steady herself. She squeezed her eyes shut and wondered if, when she opened them, she would find herself back in Aunt Ella's kitchen with that very same rocking chair and that very same teapot sitting on the long wooden table.

"The tea is almost ready, my dear," the old woman said. "Come sit down."

"Who are you?" Maddy stammered. "Where did you get that teapot? And that rocking chair?"

"Ah, Maddy, you've seen them before . . . in your own kitchen." The woman smiled gently at her confusion.

"When I was a child," she continued as she sank into the rocker, "Aunt Ella told me stories about a girl from the attic. How she came and went, always through the attic door. Aunt Ella never knew when she would appear. Or how long she would stay."

Maddy remained motionless by the door, almost unable to breathe.

"That girl was you, Maddy. I was just a wee baby the last time you arrived, and then you never returned."

For a long moment, Maddy stared at the old woman's face with its brown spots and wrinkles and its wire-rimmed glasses that enlarged the eyes twinkling back at her.

"You're Cora?"

"Yes my dear, I am Cora."

"But, you're so old!"

Cora laughed, her wrinkles deepening in her face. "A lifetime has passed since you saw me last, Maddy. My lifetime, not yours. That is still ahead of you. Full of promise too, I might add. From what I've observed, it's a good family you live with. A young family to fix up my old house and fill it with love."

Maddy's gaze flickered to the window and then back to the woman's face. Some of her features, perhaps the chin and the way she held her mouth reminded Maddy of Aunt Ella. She sounded just like Aunt Ella too. For a long, quiet moment, Maddy stood by the door, letting this unexpected and delightful discovery sink into her consciousness. She realized in her heart that both Aunt Ella and Cora were wise women and their words were true. Maddy really did live with a good family. One who loved her deeply. All day yesterday she had noticed how Dan gently cared for baby Coralee and her mom. And maybe for her. He had bought her the cell phone and downloaded her photographs without a complaint. At breakfast that morning, he grinned as he slid pancakes onto her plate and then laughed when she snapped the picture of him. He still could be crusty on the outside, as Aunt Ella had said, but when he took care of Coralee, he was soft and tender. Perhaps he'd be more patient with her, less bossy . . . if she were friendlier and more cooperative, especially about looking after Coralee.

Amy was wrong about babies. Being a big sister had its up-side . . . one she now looked forward to.

Cora patiently watched Maddy sort out her thoughts in her head for a few minutes and then pointed at the tea-pot. Maddy grinned, stepped up to the counter, and poured two cups. She handed one to Cora and placed the other on the table close by. She pulled out a chair and perched on its edge.

"You know, I named my sister Coralee after you."

"So your grandfather told me."

"Poppa George?"

"He's a good man. Very interested in my family's past."

"Yeah, he's a history nut." Maddy hesitated before she asked. "Does he know about Clare and Eva?"

"Only from the old pictures." Cora pointed at a large sepia photograph hanging on the wall.

Maddy hesitantly walked towards the framed picture. In it, a large family gathered in front of the octagon next to the porch. Maddy recognized Aunt Ella and an older Aunt Helen and Uncle Ray. A young girl with a large white bow perched on her head sat on the grass by their feet.

"Is that you?" Maddy pointed and Cora laughed.

"I was only five years old when that photograph was taken."

"Who is that man standing next to Aunt Ella?"

"Why, that's Clare!"

Maddy studied the young man's poised figure. He was even taller than the last time she had seen him. His broad shoulders stretched the suit he wore. His hair was parted on the side and neatly combed back. She hardly recognized in him the boy she knew from their time together in the mill, although he did resemble the older one who had hugged her goodbye in the barn.

"What happened to him?" she asked softly.

"After the war, he married and raised a family."

"In my house? The octagon?"

"No. In Toronto. But he visited us often."

Maddy nodded. How strange that Clare's life was the opposite of hers. That he had lived in the octagon as a boy and then moved to the city. That she was born in the city and had moved to his house in the country. For only a brief summer their lives had crossed paths, but she would never forget him. She wondered if a small piece of her heart would always ache with the loss of him.

But, somehow, in meeting Clare, she had begun to feel rooted in her new life. The octagon had begun to heal the rifts inside her—the upheaval of leaving her city friends, the confusion she wrestled with when Dan became her stepfather, the adjustment to new routines in a new place. And now, most importantly, the arrival of her sister. Maddy realized that many lives had been lived in her house. And that she and her family were now part of its history. There was something deeply satisfying in that knowledge. Something, like Poppa George once said, about being caught up in the ebb and flow of life.

As Maddy turned away from the photograph, the cat brushed up against her leg. She bent to scratch its ear.

"Did your family always name their cats Shadow?" she asked. "Like even the black one on that quilt?"

"My baby quilt? The one Aunt Ella stitched?" Cora's eyes sparkled. "Did you find it?"

"It's in an old trunk up in the woodshed. There's a doll

there too."

"I was afraid that quilt had been hauled to the dump years ago when I sold the house."

"Nope, it's still there. I think a mouse chewed a hole in it. And some of the stitches are loose. Want me to bring it over?"

Cora leaned back in the rocker. "Perhaps not. My eyes are old and my fingers are full of arthritis. It should stay in your house. Does your mother quilt?"

"She's a photographer. But she's good at decorating. I bet she knows someone who can fix it up."

Cora sighed and closed her eyes. Shadow settled in the basket by her chair. After a few minutes, Maddy wondered if the old woman had gone to sleep just like the cat. Should she go home?

She waited a few more minutes and then tiptoed past the rocking chair. The old woman reached out and placed her hand on Maddy's arm.

"Maddy, give the doll to my namesake, Coralee, and when she's older, tell her its story."

"She'll like that," Maddy whispered. "And the other stories too."

From its basket, the black cat raised its head, opened one yellow eye, and winked at Maddy.

Acknowledgments

Writing *The Girl from the Attic* has been a long and often solitary journey, except when my characters began to reveal themselves and when I shared their story, chapter by chapter, with my critique group and writer friends. I am grateful for their feedback.

When my children were young, I read them *The Root Cellar* by Janet Lunn. This tale planted a desire inside me to travel back in time and imagine the stories of those who could have inhabited my old home. Thank you.

Many years afterwards, Ted Staunton assigned our children's writers class to write the first chapter of a fantasy novel. While driving home that evening, *The Girl from the Attic* began to take shape in my mind. Later Ted graciously read it and provided very appreciated guidance that helped me reshape it at a critical point.

My neighbour Joy Gifford shared many stories about

her ancestors who once lived in the octagon. Although the characters and situations in this book are a work of fiction, their imagined lives inspired this story. Thank you.

Much appreciation is extended to my patient and meticulous editor, Emily Stewart, who challenged me to rewrite and restructure this novel to its current shape, always paying attention to even the smallest detail. Thank you for each suggestion.

Thank you to Kirsten Marion and The Common Deer Press for awarding me second prize in the 2019 Uncommon Quest Competition with the promise to publish this book, and to David Moratto for his expertise and care in designing its cover, and to Siobhan Bothwell for her work on the interior.

Last but not least, thanks is given to my husband Edward Hagedorn, who never questioned why I spent so much time over the years working and reworking each sentence. As an artist himself, he truly understands the drive and frustrations and the immense amounts of time that are poured into the artistic process. Thank you too for agreeing to illustrate the story and its cover.

About the Author

Marie Prins's life has been, in one way or another, about books. As a child she devoured them, at university she studied them and earned a BA in English Literature, and as an adult she sold them at The Toronto Women's Bookstore and Parentbooks. Now she teaches children to read them and tries to find time to write her own.

www.marieprins.ca